Ellen
Found

CARLA KELLY

Copyright © 2025 Mirror Press
Print edition
All rights reserved

No part of this book may be reproduced or distributed in any form whatsoever without prior written permission of the publisher, except in the case of brief passages embodied in critical reviews and articles. This novel is a work of fiction. The characters, names, incidents, places, and dialog are products of the author's imagination and are not to be construed as real.

Interior Design by Cora Johnson
Edited by Meghan Hoesch and Lorie Humpherys
Cover design by Rachael Anderson
Cover Model Illustration by Period Images, Pi Creative Lab and Maria Chronis.
Background: Deposit Photos #407171822 by Digidream.

Published by Mirror Press, LLC

This story was originally published as part of the Timeless Western Collection: A Wyoming Summer

ISBN: 978-1-952611-49-0

Other Works by Carla Kelly

A Naval Surgeon to Fight For
The Lady's Companion
Regency Glad Tidings
The Wedding Journey
Libby's London Merchant
One Good Turn
Where Dreams Meet
Her Smile
My Loving Vigil Keeping
The Unlikely Master Genius
The Unlikely Spy Catchers
The Unlikely Heroes
The Unlikely Gunwharf Rats
Calico Ball
A Wyoming Summer

*In loving memory of Virginia Kent,
dear friend and reader—*

the best part of writing are the people I meet

One

NINETEEN YEARS OLD. After a short lifetime of wanting little because she had nothing, Ellie Found decided she wanted more.

There it was, an ad in the *Butte Inter Mountain*. She moved the smelly fish head aside, supper for Plato the monster cat. "'For the adventurous only,'" she read out loud, then read in silence about the Yellowstone Park Association needing a kitchen girl for the crew building a hotel near Old Faithful. "'Room and board, thirty dollars a month,'" she read.

She needed a change from the Mercury Street Café. A month ago, Mr. Linson fired Addie Jackson. Ellie couldn't help overhearing. "You sassed me once too often. Get out."

Addie was gone by noon, telling Ellie,

"Leave this dump." She lowered her voice. "Don't trust 'em."

Ellie didn't.

Addie Jackson was replaced by a cook who smoked constantly, the ash from her cigarette ending up in many a meal. Revolted, Ellie still found it fascinating how ash looked like pepper in the scrambled eggs. The cook never spoke. All she did was roll another cigarette and point to the next task.

"I can't stay here," Ellie muttered as she scraped a carrot. "Get a plan, Ellen Found."

She tore out the ad and wrapped the fish head for Plato, the demon cat who barged into her life in a snowstorm and never left. Last year, when he limped toward her in the alley, she found a friend. As Ellie stared, he'd raised his afflicted paw. "Don't scratch me," she said. He yowled when she yanked out a thorn, then licked her hand and followed her into her miserable room under the Mercury Street Café.

She'd shared her dinner of soup and bread with him, explaining that he would eat when she did, and it might not be what he wanted. He curled up beside her on her cot, apparently

Ellen Found

willing to take the good with the bad, same as she did.

That was last year.

"Goodnight, Mr. Linson," she said, hoping her boss's slimy son wasn't around. He frightened her too.

"Don't be late tomorrow," Linson said. She was never late, a lesson learned from the nuns of St. Catherine's, who ran an orphanage and taught her to work hard and remember her lowly place.

Plato waited politely for her in the alley. She let him out every morning to do whatever a cat who looked like him did, but he always came back.

After a feast for Plato—of fish head, and stew and stale toast for her, Ellie reread the ad, her eyes lingering over thirty dollars a month, plus room and board. She kept reading. "'Work guaranteed until June 1904, when Old Faithful Inn opens. Continued employment possible.'"

Her letter went in the corner mailbox after breakfast. She found a stamp in the drawer under the cash register. While Linson argued with his son in the back, she addressed the envelope: *Harry Child, Yellowstone Park Association, Bozeman, Montana.*

Ellie knew better than to use the Mercury Street Café as a return address. She darted across the street to the Miners Emporium. The owner always smiled at her, so she did not fear him.

"May I use your address for this job application?" she asked, after a glance behind. She had never seen him inside the Mercury Street Café, so she knew he was wise.

He took the letter. "If a reply comes, I'll get it to you."

Ten days later, a bum palmed off a note into her hand. When Mr. Linson retreated, muttering, to his office, she hurried to the emporium. "Good luck," the merchant said, handing her a letter.

"'Dear Miss Found,'" she read later, "'We are considering several applicants. Be in my office Monday, 1 p.m., Babcock Building, corner of Babcock and Timmons.'"

Others? Was this a yes, or as near as? Was she going? *Yes*, she told herself. *I'll get that job.*

Ellie debated all weekend whether to say

Ellen Found

anything to Mr. Linson. She decided against it. Better to simply steal away.

Plato waited for her in his usual place that Sunday night. For a moment she debated whether to take him along, then knew she must. He was her only friend.

An earlier renter had left a shoddy carpetbag. She stuffed her belongings inside, including Plato. "You're not going to like this," she told him. "It's an adventure. Curl up on my clothes." In went his water bowl, and her toothbrush, hairbrush, and comb. "I don't own much, do I?" she asked. "Neither do you, Plato."

She kept her life savings—fifteen dollars—in her corset. She put six dollars of that in her pocket, knowing she needed tickets to the Northern Pacific Rail Road, then a little more to Bozeman.

Ellie closed her door quietly on the Mercury Street Café. At the depot, she spent one dollar and fifteen cents for the short line ticket. "That'll be another two dollars and fifty cents when you get there," the clerk told her. Three dollars and sixty-five cents gone so soon. She stared at her money, willing it not to shrink more.

She curled into a dark corner in the depot. The clerk ignored her. This was Butte; he had seen other hard cases.

"We're going to get that job, Plato," she said. "Butte, I have had enough of you."

Two

THE NPRR WAS late that morning, and she didn't know Bozeman. She asked an older man at the depot for directions. "Four blocks over, miss," he said, and tipped his hat. Painfully aware she was late, Ellie ran the four blocks, then down the hall to find *Harry W. Child* on door eight. She hurried inside.

A pretty lady waited, dressed impeccably, her polished shoes peeking out from under a stylish skirt. Two men sat there, one an older fellow, deep into Bozeman's *Avant-Courier*. The younger man carried a clipboard and an officious air—the interviewer, obviously.

"Miss Found?"

"Yes, sir."

He scrutinized his timepiece, and her

heart sank. *I snuck out of Butte, and I don't know Bozeman*, she wanted to say.

"Glad you could make it," he said.

The other candidate already looked smug. Ellie took a deep breath. "Thank you for this opportunity."

"Please wait outside," he said to the lady. "This won't take long." He barely glanced at Ellie. "Will it?"

Ellie knew he had already decided. She thought of her nine years working in Butte since the age of ten, with fifteen dollars, a moldy cat, and wariness to show for it. She had nothing to lose. "All I ask for is a chance." Ellie waited for the older man to leave, but he gave her a glance that took in everything from her bare head—a hat on her wages? Hah!—to broken shoes.

Ellie considered. She knew the job wasn't hers. *I will use this interview as a lesson for future interviews*, she thought. No one said she could, but she sat down.

"Found is an odd name," the interviewer commented.

"My mother was a lady of the line in Butte, who died at my birth," she said, her head

Ellen Found

high. "Her name was Ellen, last name unknown. The nuns found me, so that's my name."

The interviewer made a note on his clipboard. "This isn't much of a work history," he said, glaring at the two jobs she'd listed. Calmly, Ellie told him about working for free in the Copper King Mansion, starting when she was ten, then kitchen work in the Mercury Street Café.

"No such place, and I know Butte," the interviewer said. Newspaper Man coughed discreetly.

"It's there and it's not a good place," Ellie said. "When I saw your advertisement, I knew I could do better." This wasn't getting her the job, but the chair was comfortable.

"You cook?"

"Yes."

Plato started to purr. The man stared at the carpetbag. "There's a cat in there?"

"Yes."

"No cats in Yellowstone Park," he said in triumph. "Good day, Miss, uh, Found."

Not so fast, mister. "Plato is a mouse killer," she said firmly. "Don't tell me Yellowstone Park has no mice." She folded her hands in her lap, needing a chance where there was none, knowing that every deck of cards in the universe was stacked against her when all she wanted was to work in a safe place.

The man frowned at his clipboard. His expression neutral, Newspaper Man leaned over, wrote something, and raised one eyebrow.

The interviewer nodded as his face reddened. "Maybe we need a cat."

Ellie glanced at the older man, almost encouraged. She decided to act as though *she* had the job, and not that lady with the wonderful shoes. "Plato is amazing. Mice walk around Butte in fear and trembling."

The older man smiled, so she plunged on. "When he's full, he leaves me the extras." She didn't add there were hungry days when she almost considered Plato's generosity.

"Plato?" the interviewer asked. "Where would *you* have heard of Plato?"

The older man frowned, whether at her presumption or the interviewer's rudeness, she could not tell. "I dusted the books in the

Ellen Found

Copper King's library," she explained. "I opened *The Republic* and liked the name."

The interviewer looked toward the door, maybe wishing she would take the hint and leave. Newspaper Man left the room, and Ellie heard low voices. Clearly, he was giving the lady outside the good news of her hire. He returned and nodded to the interviewer.

The interviewer stared at his clipboard. "It won't work. You're too pretty. The crew will hang around the kitchen, and time is of the essence on this project. Sorry."

Ellie stared, amazed and a little flattered. Why not set the man straight? "You want my cat, but *I* won't do?" She took Plato out of the carpetbag and set him down. "I dare you to take two steps toward me. No man is going to hang around any kitchen where *I* work."

Plato flattened his ears and hissed when the interviewer stepped forward. Her hero crouched low, his eyes never leaving his prey. Plato's hindquarters twitched and his tail lashed back and forth. The interviewer leaped back, holding his clipboard in front of him.

"Stop, Plato!" She rubbed behind Plato's ears in that favorite spot and returned him to her carpetbag. "Let's go." She stood up.

"Not so fast, Miss Found." Newspaper Man glared at the interviewer. "We're hiring her, and Plato too."

"*Me*? You are?"

"Heavens, yes," the man said. "I'm Harry Child, president of the Yellowstone Park Company, and you're working for me."

"But that lady . . ."

"I sent her on her way." He turned to the interviewer, who stared back. "Hopkins, not one job seeker out of ten will tell you the truth. That's all we have heard from Miss Found."

"But . . ."

"That other woman? Don't you know when someone's lying?" He turned to Ellie. "Well? Are you in?"

Ellie nodded, too shy to speak.

"Room, board, and thirty dollars a month." He laughed. "And five dollars for Plato, plus kitchen scraps. Welcome to Yellowstone Park."

Ellie signed a contract for the winter. "Sir, how long is a season?"

"As long as I say it is," he replied. "Now, head over to Hotel Bozeman."

Ellen Found

"We can stay in the depot," Ellie assured him. "I wouldn't want to . . ." *Spend any more of my money*, she thought. *Suppose a season is really short?*

Mr. Child held up one finger. "Miss Found, let us come to a right understanding. *All* my hires stay there." He glanced at the interviewer, who seemed to wilt before Ellie's eyes. "Hopkins, I'll handle this." The door closed quietly.

Mr. Child handed her a voucher for a room and meals. "The Bozeman is around the corner. Settle in and be ready for an early start."

She hesitated; he noticed. "Yes?"

"Why didn't you hire that lady? She was dressed so nicely, and I know what I look like." Might as well be honest. "I told Mr. Hopkins I was a found baby and he wasn't impressed."

"Mr. Hopkins is a new hire, too, and he lacks experience."

"Yes, but—"

"I've eaten in a few Mercury Street Cafés. I hire determined people wanting to do better." He touched the contract. "I saw your determination."

She nodded, too overcome to speak because he was right.

"Alice Knight sings at the Bonanza Casino. I, uh, planted her to teach Hopkins something about hiring people." He chuckled. "And maybe learn to look inside people, and not just at nice clothes."

"I wish I had better clothes," Ellie admitted.

"No worry. Mrs. Child is creating uniforms for the Old Faithful Inn staff. She'll have something soon. It comes with the job."

"All I want is a chance."

"You have one."

Three

I can't discard this journal. Gwen might want to read it someday to know more about her dear mother. Also, I want to write about this construction, as Mr. Child's lead carpenter. We've been building the Old Faithful hotel since June. This was my chance to retrieve Gwen from Clare's sister in Helena. She didn't relinquish my child willingly, but Gwen is mine. Gwen has attached herself to Ellen Found, a quiet woman Mr. Child hired to assist Mrs. Quincy in the kitchen. She has a fearsome cat and a sweet smile. (Hers, not the cat's.)

THREE DAYS LATER, traveling in a yellow tourist stagecoach from Mr. Child's transportation company, Ellie arrived at the construction site.

They spent one night at a hotel in Gardiner, and another night at a soldiers' station inside Yellowstone Park. Even better, Ellie made an acquaintance.

Two acquaintances. She noticed the man and child in The Bozeman's lobby after breakfast. Mr. Child knew them, so she assumed he was one of the workers. That was that, at first.

It was a short walk to the depot from The Bozeman. To her delight, Ellie found an empty seat that contained a discarded newspaper. The porter offered to take her carpetbag, but stepped back when he heard Plato's rumbling growl from within.

She admired the scenery as they clacked along, reveling in unheard-of leisure, then opened the newspaper. She was deep in an article titled "American Renegade Killed. Desperate Fighting in Small Boat with Filipinos" when someone cleared his throat and Plato hissed.

"Oh, Plato," she said. There stood the man with the little girl. "Yes, sir?"

He had wonderful blue eyes and a close-cut beard as dark brown as his hair. "Pardon

Ellen Found

me, but my daughter needs to use the ladies' room. I'd rather she didn't go alone. I am Charles Penrose."

"Pleased to meet you, sir." She had heard that lilting accent before, reminding her of miners who came to the Mercury Street Café on Tuesdays when they served pasties. "I'm happy to help," she said, even though a train's lavatory was a mystery to her. "Where is it?"

He pointed to the front of the car. *I hope it's free*, Ellie thought.

"This is Gwener," he said. "*Gwener* is Cornish for Friday, her birth day. I call her Gwen." He gave his daughter a gentle push. "Go along, Gwen. The nice lady will help you."

The nice lady did. The two of them navigated the swaying car to a door with *Ladies* in gilt lettering. Inside was a small room with a sink and a cloth-roller bar. The other room contained the toilet.

Gwen came out promptly enough, her eyes wide. "Miss, you can see the tracks below!" Her words had a pleasant lilt, but it was not as pronounced as her father's.

Ellie pointed to a sign. "'Passengers will

please refrain from flushing when the train is not in motion," she read. Gwen giggled.

Ellie steadied Gwen as she returned to her seat. Ellie put away the newspaper and admired early snow on mountain peaks, far better than a dingy café in a mining town. She fed breakfast scraps to Plato, hunter of mice and scourge of people. *You're all I have*, she thought, then looked ahead to see Gwen smiling at her.

She usually never put herself forward, but Ellie beckoned to the child, who talked with her father, then made her way cautiously toward Ellie.

Plato went back into his carpetbag. Ellie patted the seat and Gwen joined her. "You have a cat? I like cats. Is he shy?"

"Hard to say."

Gwen handed Ellie a book. "Da said you might read to me. I can read, but isn't it fun to be read to?"

Ellie had no idea, but she nodded. "*Rebecca of Sunnybrook Farm.*"

"Da gives me a book on birthdays and Christmas," Gwen explained. "What do you get on your birthday?"

Ellen Found

"A year older," Ellie said, amused.

"No presents?" Gwen's eyes were wide with surprise.

"No." Ellie admired the cover, wondering how some people had so much, and others so little. "Where are you in the book?"

"I'm on chapter four. Again." She leaned closer. "Da has read this book over and over and is about to bop me on the head with it."

Ellie laughed. "I've never read it, so I won't bop your head."

Ellie read out loud to Gardiner, Montana, then on into the next day when Mr. Child directed his six workers plus Gwen onto one stagecoach, with two freight wagons following. "Park visitors use such coaches in the summer," he said, directing his remarks to his new hires.

"Crowded like whelks in a basket," Mr. Penrose said to Ellie as they sat down, his daughter on his lap. He pointed to the stone arch just outside Gardiner. "'For the benefit and enjoyment of the people,'" he read. "People are already calling it the Roosevelt Arch. The president himself dedicated it last spring, when he visited the park."

Ellie looked skeptically at the scenery,

which was less than impressive. Mr. Penrose must have noticed her expression. "Not too dramatic, is it? Wait 'til you see the geyser basin at Old Faithful."

Mr. Child motioned to him. "Let's have a meeting now, Charles. Move up."

"Coming, Mr. Child," he said. "May I leave Gwen with you?"

"Certainly. We have a book." She couldn't resist. "*Rebecca of Sunnybrook Farm*. You may have heard of it."

He rolled his eyes.

The builders conferred all morning in the four front rows. Lunch came from hampers, which Ellie organized because she decided to start earning her salary now. She helped with dinner as well, eaten at the log cabin soldiers' station beside the Gibbon River. The men grabbed fishing poles and joined the soldiers at the river, where they caught dinner.

Ellie and Gwen set the table inside the station. Soon potatoes were frying into crispy, salted rounds. The corporal tasted one. "Miss, come back often."

She protested, but they all helped with the dishes. Ellie walked with Gwen down to the

Ellen Found

Gibbon River after dishes, while Mr. Penrose watched. "Don't stray," he cautioned. "Bears are chunking up for winter, and you'd be a tempting morsel."

Ellie laughed at that. "It's no joke," he said seriously.

Very well, then. Conversation. Conversation. "What is this inn like?" she asked.

"It's huge. The foundation is massive, concrete layered over with rhyolite, a volcanic rock found here. The first two floors are lodgepole pine with the bark still on. Mr. Reamer wants it rustic, bringing the outside inside." He rubbed his hands together. "The walls are up and sturdy, and we're almost done shingling the roof. Oh, the roof. Amazing."

"It'll be done by next summer?" she asked, feeling dubious, and she hadn't even seen it.

"It has to be." He nodded toward Mr. Child, who walked with Mr. Reamer, the architect. "He'll lose his shirt to the Northern Pacific if it isn't. At least we can work indoors for the winter. You'll never believe the cold."

"I know cold," she said quietly, thinking of

her unheated room under the Mercury Street Café.

He gave her an appraising glance. "I believe you. You'll earn every penny of your salary."

"I intend to." She sensed kindness in this capable man who loved his daughter. "Same as you."

Four

October 12, 1903. I'm glad Gwen is with me. We'll do fine in this double log cabin, one of several built earlier as a possible hotel. Gwen is happy with Mrs. McTavish, who lives in the other half with her husband and son. She will watch Gwen while I work. It's a good arrangement. Gwen told me she wants to share a place with Miss Found.

THEY ARRIVED AT what Mr. Child called the Upper Geyser Basin ahead of nightfall. Ellie squinted into the gloom, seeing modest, crude buildings, all of them dwarfed by the behemoth, unfinished monster that must be the inn.

She had opened the carpetbag to give

Plato some air. Before she closed it, he sniffed, then growled. "It's sulfur," she whispered to him. "Get used to it."

"Do you always talk to your cat?" Gwen asked.

How to explain Plato to this child who had probably never felt the burden of loneliness or the reality that there was no human to help her? "He understands me."

Gwen nodded, accepting her answer as a child would. She joined her father, following him in the dark toward a log cabin. Ellie realized that she had never inquired where she would be staying. All she'd wanted was out of Butte.

Mr. Child pointed toward a larger building. The new hires moved that way. When Mr. Child looked her way, she asked, "Where do I go?"

"This way. Mind your steps."

She trailed after her employer. The path was slick with snow turning into ice. She saw small shacks and larger ones and something that looked like a machine shop. She sniffed the air and smelled freshly planed boards as they passed a larger structure.

Ellen Found

"Take my arm."

They made their way up shallow steps into a cavern. She looked up, squinting to see how tall the room was. She saw no end to it, not in the gloom of early evening. Imagine the place at midnight.

"This, Miss Found, is the lobby. It rises seventy feet or so. There are three floors, with rooms branching off from the main hall." She heard his sigh. "There's much to do."

"At least it's not snowing inside," she said finally, which made Mr. Child laugh and tease, "That's the best you can come up with?"

If he could joke, so could she, something she hadn't attempted before, not with someone who had power to hire and fire. "It was short notice." He chuckled, which she found gratifying.

"This was the big push during summer and autumn, to enclose this monster so we can finish the interior when snow falls." He gestured toward a massive stone structure. "This fireplace has four sides and four hearths." He gestured broadly. "It will be a great place to congregate."

"I imagine so," she said, hoping she didn't sound too dubious.

He lowered his voice. "I should warn you about Mrs. Quincy."

Oh dear, Ellie thought. *Please don't let the cook be a silent smoker.*

"My charming wife is a fine woman, but she has her moments. Don't we all? Adelaide decided she wanted a French chef, so Mrs. Quincy finds herself *here* instead of in our kitchen back home. She isn't particularly pleased."

Ellie reasoned that this could be worse. She stayed close on his heels, afraid that the darkness would swallow her. Ahead she saw lights under a closed door and smelled food cooking. The familiarity calmed her.

"Here it is," he said. "Mrs. Quincy will be fair, but she'd rather be back in our home kitchen."

Mr. Child opened the door to the finest kitchen ever, with the same rustic look of the dark lobby. There were two Majestic brand ranges, both bigger than the poor excuse in the Mercury Street Café; shelves with white china cups and plates; tables and benches; wooden

Ellen Found

bins probably holding flour and sugar; a coffee-bean grinder; two sinks; bags of carrots and potatoes and tins of tomatoes, beans, and corn. Ellie sighed with relief. She knew kitchens.

A woman not much taller than Ellie stopped stirring a pot of what was probably stew and turned around, wiping hair curled by the heat off her forehead. She frowned.

Don't complain yet, Ellie thought. *Get to know me.* "I'm Ellie Found," she said. "I come with a mouser."

The frown disappeared. "Very well, then," the cook said. "Close the door after you on the way out, Mr. Child. Tell your ill-begotten crew that we'll eat in half an hour."

The door closed. Ellie had the distinct impression Mr. Child was happy to leave. "Come over here," Mrs. Quincy said. "Let me see you better."

Ellie did as directed and set down her carpetbag. Through lowered eyelids, Ellie did her own appraisal. Mrs. Quincy looked like someone who had never suffered a fool gladly in her life.

"You're too pretty and the men will hang around," she said.

"I am here to cook, same as you," Ellie said, surprising herself. Hadn't Mr. Child said to be firm? The job was hers, after all. "No one ever said I was pretty either."

"You don't own a mirror?"

Ellie shook her head. Maybe mirrors were mortal sins at St. Catherine's. "I don't own anything," she said. "I have another dress and an apron. That's it."

"No one takes care of you," Mrs. Quincy said, her tone not so forbidding.

Ellie shrugged. "I'm an orphan."

"Is this your work dress?"

Oh, dear. Ellie's chin went up. "It's my best dress." Something compelled her to stick out her foot. "These are my only shoes, Mrs. Quincy. But I can prep and cook, and you won't be disappointed."

"You're forthright," Mrs. Quincy told her, but without the accusing tone this time.

"I never was, before I answered Mr. Child's ad," Ellie said. "May I let out my cat? I think he's the real reason Mr. Child tipped the balance in my favor."

ℰllen Found

"He's in your carpetbag? You may." Mrs. Quincy indicated a closed door. "That's your room. When the inn is done, it will be used for food storage. I suppose your cat will come and go as he pleases. They do that, don't they?"

Ellie picked up her bag and opened the door. She couldn't help her gasp of delight at seeing a bed already made, with a patchwork quilt and a pillow. There was a bureau with a mirror and a stand for a washbowl, complete with towels. "I've never seen anything like this," she said to Mrs. Quincy, who had followed her. "This is all for *me*?"

"I have the room next to yours. I'd call this a bit of a come down."

"Ma'am?"

"I was *the* cook in the Childs' residence in Helena," she said. Her voice hardened. "I cook plain food, and Mrs. Child wanted a French chef. I have been reassigned to outer darkness here."

If this was Mrs. Quincy's idea of outer darkness, she had obviously never set foot on Mercury Street in Butte. "It's a nice room," Ellie said cautiously.

"Our rooms are Mrs. Child's experiment

to decide what bedroom furniture and coverlets will look best in a wilderness environment. She thinks rich folks want rusticity."

"It's the nicest room I have ever seen," Ellie said simply. She saw hooks for all the clothing she didn't own, and a shoe rack for her one pair of shoes. One drawer in the bureau would suffice for her possessions. She could pull out the bottom drawer for Plato, who, like most cats, preferred hidden spaces.

"Does your cat like meat scraps?" she heard from the doorway as she lifted Plato from the carpetbag.

"He eats what I eat," Ellie said, then took another chance. "That was the condition of our association." She felt the need for this woman to understand her, if they were going to work together. "I took a thorn out of his paw and he wouldn't go away."

Mrs. Quincy smiled at that. "Set him down and follow me," she said. "I'll need you to scrape and chop more carrots for the stew. Potatoes too. Maybe an onion. We didn't know how many more workers Mr. Child would dredge up."

Ellen Found

Ellie set Plato on the bed. Mrs. Quincy returned to the cooking range for another stir and taste. Ellie got carrots from a sack and looked for a knife. Mrs. Quincy made a shooing gesture. "Don't dawdle! They'll be here before we know it!"

"I never dawdle," Ellie said. "More potatoes and onions?"

"Yes, and when you're done …" Mrs. Quincy looked Ellie over again. "How're your biscuits? I've been giving these miscreants pilot bread and they're sick of it."

"None finer," Ellie said firmly, well aware that this was a test, one she intended to pass. "Just point me to the baking powder."

Five

She talks to her cat. She's shy around men. Shingling done. Now a banquet. I ask myself if Ellen Found is making a difference, but how can that be? She's just kitchen help. I think she is more.

THE WORKERS FILED into the kitchen in thirty minutes, dutifully lining up by the serving table. No one looked excited or happy. The new arrivals hung back, so Ellie drew on all her bravery and gestured them in with a smile. Everyone made a wide berth around Plato, who stood by her and hissed.

Several of the men sniffed the air and exchanged glances. *I've got you*, she thought as she brought out a massive bowl mounded with

Ellen Found

hot biscuits. Mrs. Quincy slapped down the butter and a bowl of strawberry jam.

"Miss, put them on the table instead," someone said. "It's easier." He gave Mrs. Quincy a cautious glance.

"Good idea," Ellie said. A minute later the biscuits were on the tables where the men sat. She put two more pans of biscuits in the Majestic and started around with the coffee while Mrs. Quincy watched.

Ellie looked for Mr. Penrose and Gwen, then remembered that they lived somewhere else and probably didn't eat here. She lost sight of Plato. She eyed the Regulator on the wall and took out the next batch of biscuits when it was time. A red-haired man transferred them to the table, pan and all.

Mr. Child watched his crew with real satisfaction, then found a place. He tapped his mug, stood up, and indicated Ellie and Mrs. Quincy. "We're in good hands, men," he said simply.

They're just ordinary biscuits, she wanted to tell them. *I can make them in my sleep.* She dipped a sudden curtsy, enjoying unexpected applause.

"No one goes hungry here," Mr. Child informed the newcomers, and in saying that, he relieved Ellie's heart as well. He snagged a biscuit as the bowl went by. "Tomorrow, we'll finish the roof because we have enough shingles now." He smiled at the good-natured groans. "We'll be working inside, then. Fire up the Majestics early, Miss Found. We'll warm those nails."

Ellie leaned toward Mrs. Quincy. "Warm the nails? Why?"

"They're working outside on the roof. Warm nails keep their hands from freezing."

She stood by one Majestic and felt Plato rubbing around her ankles. "It's your turn," she said, adding more meat to his bowl, although he never minded carrots. She watched him hunker down and eat, knowing there was stew for her too, probably as much as she wanted. She opened the door to her room a crack, to make sure it wasn't a mirage. Nope.

After the last worker filed out, Ellie filled one sink with hot water from the Majestic's boiler. The dishes were already stacked on the serving table. Ellie saw the sag in the older woman's shoulders. "I can do these," Ellie told her. "You look tired."

That earned her a sharp look, then a reluctant nod. "Drain them on the serving table. It's oatmeal and applesauce tomorrow morning. I'm soaking the dried apples over there." Mrs. Quincy hesitated, then spoke. "Could there be biscuits again?"

"Yes'm."

"Be up by four-thirty to lay the fires. I won't be much later."

Mrs. Quincy went to her room. Ellie found rough sacking to spread on the serving table and put the washed crockery there to drain. She looked for Plato and found him by the slightly open door into the lobby, where he had already accumulated a pile of mouse carcasses. "Impressive," she said. "You're earning your keep."

"Gwen's right," she heard from the dark. "You do talk to your cat."

"Mr. Penrose! You startled me!"

Mr. Penrose held up his hands and a burlap sack in defense. "I come in peace with a bag of nails." He set the nails by one of the Majestics and set a metal sheet on top. "Pour these on the sheet. I'll bring more during the day. We'll have the roof over the *porte cochère* done tomorrow."

"I'll remember, Mr. Penrose."

"Call me Charles," he said. She nodded, certain she would do no such thing.

"I came for another reason too, Miss Found." She had no reason to back up, but she did. "Maybe you'd like to see why this inn is important."

"Well, I . . ."

"Come outside," he said. "It's just about that time. No worries. This was Gwen's idea, but she's asleep."

He held the massive iron-studded door open, and she shivered. Hopefully this wouldn't take too long, whatever it was.

They stood under the sweep of the *porte cochère* that would, by summer, shelter stagecoaches dropping off park visitors. "Over there."

She saw a plume of steam rising off a higher mound she had noticed when the stagecoach stopped. It was cold enough to see her breath, but *this* steam must be the breath of the gods of the underworld.

*E*llen Found

"Old Faithful erupts about every fifty-five minutes," he said. "Feel that?"

Ellie felt a rumble beneath her thin-soled shoes. The steam rose higher, then fell, then rose up again and then higher. She held her breath at the solitary majesty of this amazing sight, something that had probably played out, unseen, for more time than she could imagine. Just when she thought it must be done, the steam sank and then rose higher.

"Some of the soldiers tell the visitors that it's set to go off between nine in the morning and six at night," he said.

"Hopefully no one believes them!"

"Only the gullible."

She watched as Old Faithful rose once more, sank until only puffs of steam remained, then stopped. For a moment she forgot she was cold, worried about Mrs. Quincy, hoping this job would last, and embarrassed to think that her work dress was a disgrace, but she had nothing else. *Stop*, she told herself. *Enjoy this.*

Mr. Penrose said nothing to break the spell. He walked her back inside the cavern of the lobby, stopping at Plato's stash of dead mice. "Impressive."

"Plato never fails," she said, wondering at anyone's attention, aware that for the first time in her life, someone wanted to chat, not to order her about, but share an experience.

After he left, she regarded all the bowls drying on sacking and the cutlery jumbled together, an unwelcome, early-morning task. This was work on a larger scale than anything at the Mercury Street Café.

Here's the thing, she thought, after a glance at Mrs. Quincy's door. *I can't shingle a roof, but I can make a difference.*

She dried the bowls, then placed them around the two long tables, along with knives and spoons beside each bowl, a place for each man, so they didn't have to line up like, well, orphans. She filled the sugar bowls and placed those at appropriate intervals. The coffee mugs went down next as the Regulator's hands inched toward ten thirty.

The table was as nice as she could make it, even without napkins. She nodded in satisfaction, content to wake up in the morning to the pleasant fiction that during the night, someone had been kind enough—cared

Ellen Found

enough—to do all this for her as a welcome surprise.

It was a durable gift she had given herself since those earliest days in the Copper King Mansion when, as a child of ten, she already knew she would be the only person looking out for her. It was her daily gift to herself, and it felt fine in Yellowstone Park.

By seven o'clock, oatmeal, coffee and biscuits warmed themselves on one Majestic, with applesauce and canned milk and sugar on the table. Nails basked in welcome heat on sheet-metal trays on both ranges.

She had opened her door at five o'clock, and saw the tables set and ready. "Thank you, whoever you are," she said softly and began the day cheerfully, laying the fires and grinding coffee beans. She also prepared herself for more work than she was used to, because no one deliberately came to the Mercury Street Café for breakfast. It was the day's slowest meal.

The workers eating stew last night assured her she would be busy, but for the first time in her life, she understood the difference between work and drudgery. She was now part of this enterprise of building a hotel.

Mrs. Quincy noticed the tables. She walked around, seeing the order. "Ellie, you needn't go to all this trouble."

"I know," Ellie replied, hoping Mrs. Quincy would understand. "Mr. Child said last night how busy these men are. Let's make things easy for them in the mornings." She picked up the nearest bowl. "They can go to the range for their oatmeal, but everything else is on the table in easy reach. It will save time. I couldn't find any napkins."

"That's almost too much gentility for these ruffians," Mrs. Quincy said, but her voice was milder. "I doubt we have napkins. What are their sleeves for?"

"We can do better. Maybe there is a spare sheet somewhere? This is a hotel, after all," she added, which brought genuine laughter from her boss and gave her heart. "Some of the biscuits are warming, and two more pans are almost ready. If you can locate more canned milk..."

Everything was ready by the time Ellie heard the first boots stamping in the concrete

Ellen Found

drive. "Come in, come in," Mrs. Quincy commanded. "Take a bowl from the table and dip out your oatmeal. Plenty of biscuits too." She put her hands on her hips. "Don't stare!" She glanced at Ellie. "We decided to make things better for you."

The men went about breakfast quietly, chatting with their neighbors, holding out their mugs for more coffee when Ellie came around, never failing to thank her. When they finished, the carpenters stacked their bowls, mugs, and utensils by the sink.

"Never seen 'em do that," Mrs. Quincy whispered.

Ellie watched them each pick up a metal cup she had noticed earlier. Gloves on, they put hot nails into the cups, ran a cord through the lip of the cup, and tied them around their waists over their outercoats. Other men poured more nails onto the heated sheet as someone added a log to the Majestic.

Mr. Penrose came in after breakfast with his nail cup. "We can't wear thick gloves or we'd never be able to use a hammer well. Nobody gets frostbite with thinner gloves and heated nails."

"That's clever," she said. "Who thought that up?"

"I did."

Ellie wanted to thank him again for last night's glimpse of Old Faithful, but there was Mrs. Quincy. Better just wash dishes.

"Ellie, one more thing."

She wiped her hands on her apron. "Yes, sir?"

"My crew said they came in here to see everything already on the table. It means a lot to all of us. Thank you."

She could have mumbled her thanks and gone back to washing mugs. She couldn't, not after the wonder of Old Faithful by moonlight last night, and the kindness of the man beside her.

"You've been kind to me, Mr. Penrose," she said, "you and Gwen both. And Mr. Child too. I'll do my best work here."

"I don't doubt it," he said and joined his crew.

Mr. Child came in for coffee after the dishes were done. "Charles Penrose told me what you did this morning."

"I like things to be orderly," she said,

hoping she didn't sound silly, and remembered her request, hoping it didn't sound silly either. "Mr. Child, do you have a spare bedsheet? I want to cut it up and make napkins."

"I have a better idea," he told her. "Come with me."

Ellie followed Mr. Child into the massive cavern that would become the lobby someday. He looked through one crate and another, then pulled out tablecloths and napkins already folded and separated into stacks by the dozen.

"Use these, starting tonight. Mr. Blackstock, a vice president from the Northern Pacific, is coming to dinner." His gesture took in the vast unfinished room. "The railroad is funding this venture. I didn't think we could do anything fancy, but . . ."

Ellie heard what he was trying to say. She saw the audacity all around her of a project unlike any other, in a place suited for the unusual. "You would like a banquet tonight," she said simply. "Maybe a glimpse of what we . . ." The enterprise grabbed her and caught hold. She held out her arms for the tablecloths and napkins. "What *we* can show the public this summer."

"You have it," he said. "The soldiers are bringing elk roasts for tonight. What can you do to make it special?"

"A cake," she said with no hesitation. "Mashed potatoes. Gravy. Canned vegetables, but that can't be helped. Rolls."

"You're on, Miss Found." He started for the big doors. She could hear men stamping around on the roof over the entrance. "Six o'clock?"

She wondered how Mrs. Quincy would appreciate taking orders from her. "Yes, sir."

Six it was. The hardest part was informing Mrs. Quincy what she and their boss had agreed to. To her surprise, Mrs. Quincy merely nodded. "I'll do the meat and gravy," she said.

"I'll do rolls and a cake," Ellie added.

"Wonderful."

What had happened? It was as though a light switch—none of which were here in the hotel yet—had turned on, and her advice mattered. Ellie looked at Mrs. Quincy for explanation. What she saw was an older woman, a tired one, maybe someone who had served her own apprenticeship in a Mercury Street Café somewhere, only it had turned her

*E*llen Found

suspicious and maybe bitter. And sad about being replaced by a French cook in an elegant house. *I think I understand you, Mrs. Quincy*, Ellie thought.

So the day went. Lunch for the crew was a hurried affair eaten on the porch, potted meat and pilot bread sandwiches and plenty of hot coffee. Gwen came by in the middle of the afternoon to check up on her father, which meant Ellie took a break and joined her beyond the porch to step outside and watch the carpenters, some of whom were shingling outer walls, too.

Gwen pointed to the pinnacle, with its flat surface and railing. "Papa is up there, where he watches." She blew a kiss. Far above, Mr. Penrose touched his cheek where the "kiss" landed. "You could blow him a kiss," Gwen said. "He wouldn't mind."

Oh no. Ellie invited Gwen inside to help roll yeasty doughballs and stuff them three at a time into muffin tins. "Cloverleaf rolls," Ellie explained. No need to let anyone know that she had never made anything this elegant for the Mercury Street Café, where Mr. Linson would have berated her for wasting time on bums.

The shingling was done by four o'clock, just as the cake—Ellie's first, but no one needed to know that—came out of the oven and the first batch of rolls went in. She looked around, pleased to hear Mr. Penrose compliment his daughter on the symmetry of her doughballs.

Gwen sidled closer to Ellie. "Can we butter him one or two?"

"If he behaves," she teased. "Perhaps he can tell me something about this . . . monster, if he has a moment to spare."

"You'll hear more tonight from the architect himself," he said as Gwen handed him a cloverleaf roll. "Other ruffians, as Mrs. Quincy likes to call us, have been framing the other levels, the hotel rooms." She saw the pride as his gaze took in the men lounging on the porch, some smoking, others downing more coffee, all of them done for the day, which was quickly turning to dusk. "Soon you'll see amazing scaffolding going up inside. We'll get it done."

He indicated the small man with gold-rimmed glasses who stood at the entrance to the lobby, a clipboard under his arm. "Mr. Reamer is in charge. See? He has a clipboard."

Ellen Found

She thought about clipboard efficiency, as she iced the sheet cake after Mr. Penrose left. "No, Plato, I have never made a cake before, and I don't have a clipboard," she told her cat, who lounged between the warmth of both Majestic ranges. "But I can read a cookbook, and you can't."

Plato didn't seem to give the matter much thought. He rolled onto his back as if to announce, *I am full of mice*. "Don't concern yourself," she added, then laughed when Mrs. Quincy regarded her. "Yes, ma'am, I talk to my cat. He's my friend."

"I'd say that Mr. Penrose and his daughter are your friends."

She could blush and deny and keep her head down, but why? Something was changing in her. Maybe she could blame it on geysers. "I hope they are my friends." And why not? "You too, Mrs. Quincy."

Six

Great banquet. Ellen Found is even more of an asset than Mr. Child realized when he hired her. She has a quiet way of taking charge. I doubt she is aware of it, but I am.

"THEY TUCKED IN their shirttails," Mrs. Quincy whispered to Ellie. "Even One-Eyed Wilson."

The builders congregated in the dining room, sneaking peeks at the mounds of mashed potatoes, gravy with no lumps, boring canned peas, stewed tomatoes with chunks of bread, and rolls glistening with butter. To her surprise, Mr. Penrose and Gwen were among the guests.

Ellen Found

Brought by soldiers from Fort Yellowstone, the elk roast took up considerable real estate on the next table. Excellent. Mr. Child wanted elk, and here it was. Somehow even the heavy China plates and bowls looked elegant.

The door opened and Mr. Child and Mr. Blackstock, his railroad guest, entered, swiping at the snow on their overcoats. Mr. Child was joined by Rob Reamer, the architect, who looked at the tables and nodded as if this sort of thing happened every day.

Mr. Child took the arm of a commanding-looking woman wearing a hat too frivolous for a snowy day. Mrs. Quincy whispered, "Mrs. Adelaide Child herself, the law-dee-daw lady who threw me over for a French chef."

"Her loss," Ellie whispered back. "Let's serve dinner."

Mrs. Quincy had argued for a separate table for the dignitaries, but Ellie had quietly and kindly overruled her. To her relief, she was right, watching with satisfaction to see the railroad executive in animated conversation with the one-eyed roofer. The architect appeared in deep conversation with a German in charge of steam boilers, soon to provide electricity.

She wasn't prepared for Mr. Child to gesture *her* over. Mrs. Quincy gave her a prod in the back, and she found herself under the scrutiny of *the* Mrs. Child.

"This is the resourceful miss who is adventurous," Mr. Child told his wife. "She is also responsible for tablecloths for my workers' breakfast." He smiled. "I hear they were suitably impressed!"

"Do you do that every morning?" Mrs. Child asked. To Ellie's relief, she sounded genuinely interested.

"Yes, ma'am," Ellie replied. "To me, it's a . . . a rehearsal of what this hotel will look like in June."

Silence. Worried, Ellie glanced at Mr. Child and saw his approval. "Keep doing this," he said. "We need to understand what a great enterprise looks like." He turned his attention to the serving table. "Do I see *cake*?"

"You do, sir," Ellie said. She understood cake, but she had never attempted piping on little rosettes before, done with a pastry bag

Ellen Found

made of rolled, stiff paper. Maybe no one would look too closely at the writing.

Mrs. Child came closer. Ellie held her breath, hoping it would survive the scrutiny of someone like Mrs. Child, who had a French chef.

"'Old Faithful Inn,'" Mrs. Child read. "You should have piped on our geyser."

"All I had was red food coloring," Ellie said and couldn't help a smile. "It would have looked like a burst artery."

Everyone laughed, a good-hearted, we're-in-this-together sound. The cake slices went around, and all was well.

"Better look out, Ellen," Mr. Penrose said when he picked up two plates. "Mrs. Child might nab you for her mansion in Helena."

"I won't go," she said, her face warm. "I like it here where I have . . ." She looked at him, admiring his blue eyes and frank face. "Friends."

"Count me among them," he said.

To Ellie's surprise, when the meal was over, everyone except the guests cleared the table. She and Mrs. Quincy headed for the kitchen, but Mr. Child stopped them. "That will keep. Please join us. Mr. Penrose, there's an empty chair next to you."

She sat, too shy to look at the boss carpenter, but happy to smile at Gwen. Mr. Penrose leaned closer. "Bravo, Miss Found. *You* are an event planner, obviously."

"No . . . I . . ."

"Papa is right," Gwen said. "I wouldn't argue."

"I won't," she whispered, stifling her laughter.

"Mr. Reamer, the floor is yours," Mr. Child said.

The architect pushed his glasses higher on his nose. He turned to an easel and put up an artist's rendition of the inn at Old Faithful. He took his listeners through dismal years of poor lodging—one was actually called the "Shack Hotel"—and bad food at one of the world's most amazing places.

"Mr. Blackstock, earlier impresarios didn't dream big enough," he said, addressing the railroad executive. "What we have in Yellowstone are forests and geysers and hot pots and utter magnificence."

*E*llen Found

"Otter magnificence," one of the workers called out. "I saw some in August!"

It was the perfect, spontaneous touch. Everyone laughed and suddenly seemed to own the project. Ellie felt it inside her. Mr. Reamer relaxed; he must have felt it, too. "What I am doing with this . . ."—he gestured toward the dark cavern beyond the dining room—"otter magnificence"—more laughter—"is bringing the outdoors indoors."

More renderings appeared, one showing fanciful woodwork made of twisted lodgepole pines that in other projects might have been discarded. "Let the forest speak, I say," Mr. Reamer told his audience. He raised his pointer toward the ceiling in the next room. "Whimsical dormer windows here and there will mimic the play of sunlight in our wonderland."

Mr. Reamer continued, after a dramatic pause. "No one will come to this inn, experience our hospitality, and leave without an appreciation of what we have to offer the world. Yes, the world." He paused again for dramatic effect, then pulled out the final rendering, a completed hotel. "Old Faithful

Inn will set the standard for all national park lodging. Thank you."

He sat down. Mr. Blackstock broke the silence, pulling out a check and waving it. "Will this help?" he asked. "The Northern Pacific Railroad believes in you!"

Everyone rose and applauded. Mr. Penrose put Gwen to his shoulder and stood. The child looked around with sleepy eyes, then nestled against her father again. Ellie felt the loveliness of a moment only she witnessed. All other eyes were on Mr. Child and the railroad executive, as he handed over the check that would complete the project.

"June first!" Mr. Blackstock proclaimed.

That was everyone's signal to leave the powerful men alone to talk. Mr. Penrose walked among the workers who followed him into the kitchen, rolled up their sleeves, and started on the dishes.

Mr. Penrose looked around. "Is there somewhere I can put Gwen?"

Ellie opened the door to her room. "She'll be fine here."

"Posh digs, Miss Found," he teased, looking around in appreciation. "I like it."

Ellen Found

"I've never lived anywhere so wonderful in my life."

Maybe she was too fervent. Mr. Penrose gave her such a look, the sort of look she knew she would remember forever. He set his child down and Ellie covered her with a light blanket. "You're right," he said. "It's a nice room."

"You can't imagine," Ellie told him.

"Maybe I can. Kindly call me Charles." He smiled. "So I can call you Ellen."

"Everyone calls me Ellie."

He shrugged. "I like Ellen."

The dishes were soon done. With a red-haired roofer's help, Ellen turned over two mostly clean tablecloths and set the breakfast table. "I wish it could be something besides oatmeal," she told Red Hair.

"Convince ol' Harry Child to get us some laying hens," he said. "I'm a tenant farmer from County Cork." Ellen smiled at his wonderful accent.

"Add a pig or two," chimed in One-Eyed Wilson. He nudged the other man. "We have enough shanty Irish working here not to mind a pig in the bunkhouse!" Red Hair glared at him.

"I can convince ol' Harry."

Ellen turned to see Mrs. Child, who raised her eyebrows as the strong men cowered. The two men quietly melted into the gang finishing the cleanup.

"Let me see your room," Mrs. Child said. She made a face. "The men's bunkhouse is a disaster! They scattered like rats when I came in."

Mr. Child joined her. "They weren't expecting you, Adelaide. And you forgot to knock."

Ellen kept a straight face only through years of being a servant who, she had been informed by the copper king's wife, was never to be seen *or* heard. "This way, Mrs. Child," she said, and put a finger to her lips. "There is a sleeping child."

She opened the door to see Mr. Penr—Charles—picking up his still-sleeping daughter. "Thanks for the loan of your room," he whispered.

Mr. Child and Charles conversed quietly in the doorway while Mrs. Child surveyed the

Ellen Found

room. She jiggled the mattress. "Firm, but not too firm." Mrs. Child pointed to the hooks in the wall, where Ellen's other dress, the sadder one, hung. "You should hang up all your dresses."

"This is all I have," Ellen said, head up but cringing inside.

Mrs. Child turned to her husband. "Harry, I have a wonderful idea."

"Yes, my dear?"

"I've decided to speed up my plans for hotel uniforms."

"Yes, my dear."

"Ellie will be my model. I'll be here tomorrow with my tape measure," she announced, then followed her husband and a grinning Charles Penrose out the room.

Mrs. Quincy joined her. "'Yes, my dear,'" she teased. "In case you wondered who wears the pants in that family." Her voice hardened. "I only wish she had been nicer to me."

"Maybe she regrets it."

"Do you give everyone the benefit of the doubt?" Mrs. Quincy asked as she opened the door to her own room.

Do I? There's no harm in that, she

thought. *It's all I want.* "I suppose I do," she replied.

She searched for Plato and found him crouched over another mouse carcass in the pitch-dark lobby. "I saved some crispy elk pieces for you."

"Any for me? I like crispy bits too."

Funny how she already recognized his voice. "Mr. Penrose—"

"Charles."

Hands on hips. "Mr. Penrose, you're too quiet!"

"I learned that after Gwen was born," he said. "Let sleeping children lie. She's in her bed, and I come at Mrs. Child's request. Well, perhaps her command."

"Look out for Plato."

Plato hissed. "Is it men he doesn't like, or is it everyone except you?"

"Everyone," she said, enjoying the mild banter. "What does the lady want?"

"I am to measure your foot for shoes."

"I . . . suppose she couldn't help seeing . . . I could use some good shoes." It was true. Why protest? Everyone knew it, including this man with kind eyes.

Ellen Found

"Take off your shoe and stand on the paper."

She did as he said and stepped on the sheet. He grasped her ankle and outlined her foot. "Mrs. Child is observant," she said, keeping her voice light, wanting to cut the odd tension.

"Not her," he said quietly. "Me."

The nuns had warned her about predatory men years ago. But as she stood there, one shoe on, one off, Ellen knew this man was no predator. She knew that she had fallen among friends.

"Thank you, Mr. Penrose."

"Charles," he reminded her. "You'll have shoes. Winters are cold here." He nodded toward the door, perhaps wanting to change the subject. "Feel that rumble?"

She followed him outside to the porch, rubbing her shoulders against the cold, to watch Old Faithful erupt.

Ellen watched, thinking of cold men on a steep roof. "Thank goodness the roof is done."

"We'll finish the inside this winter." He sniffed the cold air. "Not a minute too soon."

He nodded to her as if she mattered. "Goodnight, Ellen. You will have shoes."

Seven

Morning coffee with Ellen. Can I tell you, dear journal, how nice that is? I had almost forgotten.

THE SHOES ARRIVED three weeks later, along with uniforms. Since she was cutting up onions, her tears needed no explanation.

"Try them on now." Mrs. Quincy looked around. "Be sure to close your door! The builders are indoors and drop in at all hours for coffee and whatever else they can scrounge."

What a change three weeks had brought. Mr. Schmitz's "Vee vill haff electricity" came true. Three steam boilers, brought earlier in August, were encased in their own building behind the inn, voraciously scarfing down all the lodgepole pines that woodcutters produced. The steam powered the generators and produced electricity. Power tools and lifts went into action.

Inside the lobby, more scaffolding went up, which entertained Plato mightily. Now he could climb the scaffolding and threaten carpenters nailing narrow split logs high above the floor, covering the ceiling to match the walls below.

Now she had dresses. Ellen's cautious mind had told her that Mrs. Child didn't really mean it, but here they were, wrapped in brown paper.

She spread the two outfits on her bed, dresses sewn to her specifications alone. Sensible black brogans came from the box, plus six pairs of stockings. "I have never had six of anything, Mrs. Child," she murmured.

Which outfit first? Practical to the end, she pulled on the no-nonsense dark blue muslin, with its long sleeves and buttons at the wrist so she could tug them to elbow-length while working.

She buttoned up the front, pleased how

Ellen Found

well the bodice fit. The brown paper also held two petticoats. Wordless, she held them against her face. She was too shy to open a smaller package that might, just might, be what she wore under her petticoat. She tore off a corner and put her finger inside. Was this *silk*?

The other proposed uniform was a brown skirt and a green and white checked shirtwaist. She slipped on one of the two new petticoats first, then buttoned up the shirtwaist. The skirt brushed the top of her new shoes. She smoothed it over her hips, enjoying the feel of good material. Next came an apron, looking more like a pinafore, frilled along the bib. She patted the pocket and gasped as she pulled out a lacy brassiere.

Mrs. Quincy had to see this. She opened her door and tucked the brassiere behind her back quickly because two roofers from the highest portion of the interior roof had come for more heated nails. They grinned at her; maybe she hadn't hidden the brassiere in time.

Back it went into her pocket, just as Charles Penrose came inside for nails.

Ellen amazed herself by twirling around for him, stopping when he applauded.

He held out his tin cup for nails. "Shoes, too?"

Ellen raised her skirt to show him.

"I'm relieved," he teased. "Now you can run fast and not become a meal for bears bulking up for hibernation."

"Charles!" she exclaimed, and he laughed. "I . . . I think the blue dress is for daily wear, and the brown skirt and shirtwaist is for special events, which I don't need now. Should I return the skirt and shirtwaist, Mrs. Quincy?"

"Not on your tintype," her kitchen boss said firmly. "You are now the owner of two new dresses."

Well-dressed and enjoying it, Ellen unpacked crates of canned food, as welcome to her as the venison and moose meat now hanging in the temporary meat locker, a washroom locked and cold, safe from bears still nosing about, wondering where to hibernate.

As the days passed, Ellen began to look forward to Charles Penrose every morning before breakfast. "You make good coffee, and I don't," he said.

*E*llen Found

If she started earlier on the biscuits, she had time to sit with him. While he sipped and relaxed, Ellen started asking him what he planned for the day, which seemed to please him. "You're interested in everything," he told her one morning.

"Does that make me nosy?"

"It makes you smart," he replied, which gratified her more than the neat rows of canned beans, corn, carrots, and tomatoes.

You have a fine smile, Mr. Penrose, she thought, after he nodded to her and returned to his quarters to ready Gwen for her day next door with the McTavishes.

She wished Charles would bring Gwen by for supper, then reminded herself that they ate with the McTavishes. She wanted to tell him how nice the mezzanine looked—and how much safer it was—now that the railings were in place. She reminded herself that he had a life outside of Old Faithful Inn.

He didn't come the next morning. She walked from the dining room to the lobby's entrance, assuring herself that she wasn't looking for Charles Penrose. Just curious. That was all.

There he stood, looking out at the geyser field in front of the hotel. "Mr. Penrose?" she asked, uncertain. "I made you some biscuits." She hoped that wasn't brazen. "Is something wrong?"

"I need a favor," he said, "if you think you can."

Well, that is a novelty, she decided as they walked inside. Usually, people told her what to do. No one asked.

"It's this: Mrs. McTavish is expecting another child and the post surgeon from Fort Yellowstone says she needs to leave right now. She has pleurisy that will only get worse as winter moves in."

"Poor lady. Her husband is your chief assistant, isn't he?"

"Aye. Jim tendered his resignation last night. What a blow. Well, a double blow. I've lost my right-hand man and the lady who watches my daughter."

She knew what he needed, and she knew her answer. "Charles, Mrs. Quincy and I can watch Gwen right here." She decided not to imagine what her boss might *really* think. "She can help us in the kitchen."

Ellen Found

She saw the relief in his expressive eyes. "When did *you* start peeling potatoes?" he asked, making a little joke of his concern.

She understood. "I was ten. We were taught to earn our keep young." *And remember our place and never make a wave*, she reminded herself. *Gwen will never need those lessons.* "See? Problem solved."

Sensing there was more, she waited for him to speak. "My wife, Clare, died two years ago when Gwen was four."

"So young," she said.

"Both of them." He eyed the Regulator on the wall. "Got a minute?"

"I'll stop the clock's hands if I have to. Tell me." He needed to talk and she wanted to listen.

"Clare's sister in Helena invited me to move in with her and her husband, and we did. I never have trouble finding work. I answered that same ad you did and started work here last May. Mr. Child put me in charge of the carpenters, and I answer directly to Mr. Reamer."

"I knew you had a lot of responsibility."

"Trouble came when I told Amanda I was

taking Gwen along, too. She told me I was crazy to do that and an unfit parent."

"Which you are neither."

"Thanks," he said with a brief smile. "Amanda has no children. She pleaded with me to leave Gwen with her. I can't. Gwen is mine. Mine and Clare's. It's hard though. Can you clear it with Mrs. Quincy?"

Ellen knew she had no power or standing. What was she thinking? "I will," she said firmly. "We'll do fine."

Where was her courage coming from? Maybe from the quiet man with heavy responsibilities and a small child. *I like this man*, she thought. The feeling was novel, and she wanted it to linger.

She had another thought. "I wish we could offer Gwen wages. Women need money of their own. At least, I always wanted that."

She felt he was measuring her in that same way she had seen him stare at a board before he started to saw. "How about you offer Gwen one dollar a week, which I will slip to you on the sly?"

"Done," she said. "Bring her over. See how easy that was?"

ℰllen Found

She meant it as a joke. He appraised her again, serious. "A mere thank-you is inadequate."

If Mrs. Quincy had objections when Ellen approached her about it, she stifled them. "We can use her help," was Ellen's clinching argument.

"I believe we can, Ellie," was all she said. "You're in charge of her."

Gwen and her father came over after breakfast when Mr. Reamer gave the crew his daily list of projects. Charles helped Gwen off with her coat, kissed her cheek, and went about his business for the day.

"We have a lot of potatoes," Ellen said, kneeling down. She found a potato peeler. "Let me show you how to peel them."

The child nodded. "I'll miss Mrs. McTavish and her little boy," she said, taking the peeler and looking it over.

"They'll be better off in a warmer climate, and she won't cough so much."

Ellen sat her down at the table and brought over a bowl of scrubbed potatoes. "We'll work together," she told the child. She glanced at Mrs. Quincy, who, to her surprise, watched them with an expression she might be tempted to call tender, were this anyone but Mrs. Quincy.

This turned into a day of surprises. Charles had said his daughter still liked a nap. After lunch, when Gwen started tugging on her eyelashes, Ellen took Gwen to her room, removed her shoes, and covered her with a blanket. When she came back later to check, Plato had curled up with Gwen.

"Good for you, Plato," she whispered. "Every lady needs a bodyguard."

Gwen made sure her father had an extra serving of mashed potatoes that night. "I mashed these," she announced.

He hugged her. "Never better." He smiled at Ellen. "Thank you. I know Gwen is in good hands."

She saw how tired he was, how tired they all were. Until the newly built fireplace was ready, the lobby was still going to be cold. Even working indoors was no proof against Yellowstone in the winter.

He helped Gwen with her coat. "We'll be eating here now, since the McTavishes are gone. I'm no cook."

Ellen Found

"He isn't," Gwen agreed.

Ellen walked with them through the dark lobby. Charles stopped when his daughter stooped down to pet Plato, who had come up silently beside the child. "Uh . . . careful."

"He's my friend," Gwen said.

Charles held out his hand slowly. Plato sniffed but did not hiss, and turned away. "He'll be your friend too, Papa," Gwen assured him. "I know it. Give him time."

Give me time too, Ellen thought.

Eight

Life and death can turn on a dime. I owe Ellen more than I can ever repay. More later.

GWEN PENROSE PROVED a welcome addition to the "kitchen staff," as her father described them. When the cook scoffed, he wagged a finger at her. "Mrs. Quincy, when I work with one other carpenter, it's the two of us. When I add another, it's a crew. Staff sounds nicer for ladies."

Ellen could tell when Mrs. Quincy was amused by how hard she tried not to show it. "You might as well add Plato to the staff," she replied, which made Gwen nod seriously.

With the men working inside the inn, the whole building reverberated with noise that

Ellen Found

Mr. Reamer stated was music to his ears. "June is coming, so the louder, the better," the architect announced after breakfast one morning.

Interested, Ellen stood in the kitchen doorway as Charles Penrose took everyone through the day's tasks. The architect was there too, sketching designs and plans on the underside of leftover shingles. When he finished, the shingles went into the kitchen ranges.

"By the end of next week, every room on each floor will be roughed in," Charles told her as they finished their morning coffee. "We'll close the big doors off the second-floor mezzanine and finish those rooms after the lobby is done."

As if aware of the need, winter held itself at bay, teasing with snow flurries and an overnight addition of a few inches, easily swept away from the porch and off machinery. Plato remained ever vigilant, perhaps mindful in his cat brain that cold weather meant mice were seeking warmer shelter too.

"You're getting a bit of a belly on you," she told him one night, as she prepared to blow out the light in her glorious bedroom. Plato assumed his usual place, curled up by her feet. He still ignored the men who trooped in and out of "his" hotel, hammering and sawing, but he didn't hiss at them. *Even alley cats can change*, Ellen thought. *Maybe someday he'll let Mr. Penrose pet him.*

She felt herself changing, too. At the Mercury Street Café, her usual morning routine was a quick swipe at her hair and then an old shoestring to pull it back. If she could fix Gwen's hair into French braids every morning, she could do hers, too.

She didn't think anyone noticed, but Charles Penrose did. She saw it in his eyes, which pleased her more than words. Corporal Dan Reeves of the Old Faithful soldier station noticed too. One morning he gave her a string of Indian seed beads. "You could weave these in," was all he said, but it warmed her heart for a week.

On orders from Major Pitcher, acting superintendent at Fort Yellowstone, Dan and his three privates took over a corner of the hastily built boardinghouse, closer than their regular soldiers' station. Mr. Reamer made

Ellen Found

note of the addition. "They're here to protect us from bears and poachers," he announced one morning after breakfast.

Maybe it was the good coffee and biscuits. Maybe it was the tablecloths, or even the warmth from the two Majestic ranges. No one rushed off in silence anymore. "Things are different now," Mrs. Quincy said, and Ellen heard no irritation.

"Plato, we have landed in a good place," she announced one night as he turned around a few times on his woolen square that Gwen had given him and plumped down on her bed.

Ellen sighed with contentment, thinking of the chaotic order around them as twisted tree limbs, cast-offs of lodgepole pines, filled in the spaces below the handrails on the stairways up from the lobby. "Nature is naturally chaotic," Mr. Reamer said one morning. "Visitors want the rustic experience. Here it is."

Other chaos came home one morning when, elbow-deep in bread dough, Ellen heard shouts and carpenters running. She looked around, but there was Plato, slumbering between the warm Majestics, not guilty of a single hiss.

Followed by Gwen, she opened the glass-paned door between the lobby and the dining room when someone shouted, "Hey, bear! Hey, bear!"

She slammed the door, her arms tight around Gwen, as a bear charged down the hall, picked up speed, and raced across the lobby to the open front door. He was a blur followed by men with brooms, who slammed the door after him and laughed nervously.

"We found him all snug in his bed for a warm winter's nap in one of the rooms at the end of this hall," a carpenter said and pointed when she opened the dining room door just a crack this time.

Charles Penrose came on the run. He pulled all the men off the lobby to shore up the wall where the determined bear had worried open a spot to crawl through. "Let's go around again, men," he said. "Let's be certain. I'll sleep better when every bear is denned up away from here."

For a week Ellen opened that door cautiously, which made One-Eyed Wilson laugh at her. "It wasn't a big bear," he assured her.

Ellen Found

"He looked huge," Ellen said, with all the dignity she could muster.

Maybe the bear *wasn't* so big. She took the crew's good-natured ribbing in stride, but welcomed every degree that the thermometer dropped, driving bears away to their wintertime sleep, once they had eaten everything in sight.

"Maybe I'm a goof," she told Gwen a week later as she bundled up the child for their walk to the log cabin where she and her father "batched it," as Corporal Reeves said.

Charles had asked if Gwen could stay with her until seven, because he had a meeting with Mr. George Wellington Colfitt, blacksmith from Livingston, who had braved the cold and snowy roads with two iron workers to bring his own plans for a makeshift forge here.

She assured Charles she could walk Gwen to his cabin, not so many steps from the back entrance. "I'll walk you back," he said.

She wanted to tell him that wasn't necessary. All he had to do was stand in the open doorway and watch until she was inside the lobby again. Still, it was a nice gesture.

She handed Gwen a packet of meat and

cheese from the supper that Charles had skipped. "You know, just to tide him over until breakfast."

By now, she knew her way in daylight or gloom, but something was off in the lobby. She stopped and sniffed, wrinkling her nose against an unfamiliar odor, wondering about that meat and cheese.

The bear came at them from behind, snuffling, moving fast, and chunky from eating everything in sight. She stopped, its outline barely visible because of a sliver of moonlight from the randomly placed dormer windows overhead, the ones calculated to bring the outdoors indoors. The outdoors indoors . . .

She grabbed Gwen, but there was nowhere to go. The bear, much closer, came between them and the dining room door. The outside door looked farther and farther away as the seconds passed. They were stuck. The bear kept moving.

"Toss him the meat packet," Ellen whispered to Gwen.

Misunderstanding her, Gwen threw the packet as hard as she could into the bear's face. It reared up, roared, and charged.

Ellen Found

Gwen screamed and screamed as Ellen snatched her up and backed toward the stairs. She knew she couldn't outrun an angry bear up the stairs, but they were suddenly desperate, two people out of their element in bear world.

She grabbed Gwen tighter and darted under the stairs instead. Kneeling, she shoved Gwen against the bottom step, forcing her as far in as she could go, and crawled after her. Cramped into the tight space, she threw her arms around Gwen and covered her with her own body.

To her horror, the bear crawled after them. Thank God he was too big, too bulked up for winter. He growled and swiped at Ellen's back, ripping through her dress and scoring her shoulder. As blood dripped from her shoulder, she cried out in pain and tried to make herself smaller.

The bear wouldn't stop. Blood meant food. He swiped at her skirt and managed to hook a claw in it. He tugged as Ellen clung to Gwen and tried to wrap her arms around the bottom rung. She sobbed as the bear inched her out farther. To let go and save Gwen? She had no choice.

Through the bear's deep breathing and Gwen's screams, Ellen heard Plato growl—Plato, who had vanished after supper to gnaw on mice somewhere. *No, Plato, no*, she thought as the bear tugged at her skirt.

The fiercest tomcat who ever roamed the mean streets of Butte growled and hissed. She had heard him warn away stray dogs and hiss at carpenters. This was different. This was the sound of life or death, and she knew it.

The bear grunted, then roared in pain. Looking behind her, Ellen saw Plato leap on the bear's head and claw at its eyes, an impossible task for a cat too small to fight a bear, a cat possessing nothing but puny claws and a heart so big that even the lobby couldn't contain it. "Plato, run," she whispered. "Please. *Please.*"

With a roar that echoed off the distant ceiling, the bear grabbed her cat, chomped down, and flung what remained against a far wall. Tears streamed down her face as Ellen clapped her hand over Gwen's mouth and held her tight against her body.

She waited for the bear to grab at her again. When it didn't, she looked over her

Ellen Found

shoulder at the beast to see it rubbing its eyes where Plato had clawed and bit. The bear whimpered, distracted, unsure.

After years and years, she heard the back door slam open. She watched, dull with pain of the heart worse than the claw marks on her back, as Corporal Reeves went to one knee, took deliberate aim, and fired. The noise reverberated in the huge room and her ears rang. He fired again and once more until the bear lay still.

Ellen felt herself pulled gently from that too-small space. Some primitive reflex made her cling tenaciously to the little girl, even though the more rational part of her brain assured her the ordeal was over. Someone carefully pried her fingers from Gwen, then kissed her hand.

"Ellen, my debt to you is eternal," she heard before she closed her eyes and wept.

Nine

Ellen Found is resilient, but such loss! I have only a glimmer of how sad she is. What can I do?

SHE WOKE UP MERE MINUTES later, clawing and scratching to hang on to Gwen, who was clasped tight in her father's arms. Corporal Reeves held her in a sitting position as Mrs. Quincy, her face white and her eyes huge, dabbed at her back with a dishcloth.

Lanterns and men filled the space close to the stairs, and it was light enough for her to really see the bear. Just an ordinary bear, but a big one, a bear looking for one last meal before the long winter's sleep.

Ellen looked harder against the distant

Ellen Found

wall. She sobbed when she saw the ridiculously small bundle of fur and bones that had taken on a behemoth in the Old Faithful Inn lobby. "Please, someone get Plato. Please."

One of the privates followed her shaking finger. He knelt, then called to another soldier, who went into the dining room and returned with a dish towel. Carefully he wrapped it around the little body and carried Plato to Ellen, who held out her arms.

"He's still alive," the private said. "Not for long."

Time, merciful time, stood still long enough for her to cradle the demon cat of Butte and smooth down his torn and bleeding fur. "Plato, you should've run the other way," she whispered to her friend, her only friend ever. She had helped him out of his pain in the alley, and he returned the favor moments ago by distracting a monster many times his size and saving two lives. "You thought you were a mountain lion, little buddy," she said. "And here we were at last, with enough food to eat and a safe place to sleep."

Mr. Penrose made a little sound when she said that, or maybe it was Corporal Reeves.

She wept over her dying cat, smoothing his fur. Plato put a delicate paw on her wrist finally, as if to say, "That'll do, my lady friend. I'm all right now. You're here." To her stunned amazement, he started to purr and then he died. She marveled that such a small body could hold something as enormous as death, then fainted.

Ellen woke in her own room, wearing her flannel nightgown with most of the flannel gone, her left shoulder throbbing and wrapped in a bandage. His face a study in agony, Charles Penrose sat on her bed, his daughter asleep in his arms but crying out at intervals.

From habit, Ellen looked toward her feet, but there was no Plato, only his wool square. Charles's eyes must have followed hers. "I wrapped him in a towel," he said, his voice strained. "I have a carved wooden box in my quarters. I will bury him in a good place."

"Please put in Gwen's wool square," she said. "He liked to sleep on it."

"I will."

He didn't leave, not even when Mrs. Quincy came into her room with something sweet and chocolatey, something Ellen saw the children in the Copper King house drink, but which she was not allowed. She took a sip and another, knowing that Plato would have liked it, too. She took tiny solace remembering that for dinner that night, there had been plenty of stewed tomatoes and bread chunks, something Plato loved.

"My shoulder?" she asked, not sure who would answer and not wanting to think that Mr. Penrose had to get her out of the tattered dress. Her back felt on fire.

"There was one deep scratch."

"Who fixed my shoulder?"

"The one-eyed man, name of Fred Wilson, and Mrs. Quincy helped. He's a good carpenter and maybe a better taxidermist. Miss Found, you have a neat row of stitches as nice as anything I've ever seen. He does good work."

She shook her head at that and felt an absurd urge to smile, maybe even laugh. Charles watched her. "Ellen, he said it was the best row of stiches he ever put in anything." He patted her hand, and she realized he was holding it. "He said you were museum quality."

She laughed, just a small laugh, a tentative

one, the sort of laugh that maybe a person tries out who is wondering why she is even alive. She looked at the sleeping child in her father's arms. "You hold her tight tonight," she said, not meaning to sound so adamant. "For as long as she needs you." *Who will hold me?* remained unspoken. Her only friend was gone.

"I had better leave," Charles said.

"Where is . . ." She couldn't even say his name.

"Plato's in the room where we hang meat," Mrs. Quincy said.

"I'll do what you want and bury him tomorrow," Charles told her. "I know a good place." He walked to the door, his arms tight around Gwen, and stood there a long moment. "I am truly in your debt." He tried to say more but shook his head instead and left.

Mrs. Quincy stood by her bed, the torn dress over her arm. "Mrs. Child is going to be so disappointed in me," Ellen said. "I wish I had been wearing my old dress."

Her eyes intense, her boss plumped down on the bed. "Ellen Found, Mrs. Child is going to be so relieved—as we are—that you had a champion defending you! Don't you dare worry about your dress. I can sew the tear, and you'll wear it again."

And not think about Plato? she asked herself. She nodded, feeling the tug of gravity on her eyelids. Was it even possible to sleep after the terror of this evening? She knew when she closed her eyes, maybe every time she closed her eyes, she would see that enormous bear rising on its hind legs. Maybe she would feel its hot breath on her neck as she struggled to make herself small under the stairs and keep Gwen covered with her body. Or maybe she would just sleep, which was what happened.

More than once, though, she woke in tears during the night, feeling for Plato, who liked to migrate north from her feet to curl up next to her shoulder in cold weather. She thought she heard him purr, which sent her back to tears and then to sleep.

Through it all, she was aware that Mrs. Quincy never left her, but sat on the floor beside her bed, her hand on Ellen's good arm. She even hummed once, a tune Ellen had heard one night passing a honky-tonk on Mercury Street. "Sweetest little fella, everybody knows . . ." She wiped Ellen's eyes when she cried and said, "Shh, shh, shh," softly.

Morning came as it always did. Ellen was aware that Mrs. Quincy had left, and she heard low voices, then the rattling of wood into the Majestics. Breakfast was going to come as it always did, no matter how dead Plato was or how her shoulder ached. She reminded herself that she was earning thirty dollars a month and sat up.

Her entire body ached, from the tousled hair on her head to her toenails. She moved her arm tentatively, pleased to discover that she could even move it. It pained her greatly, so what did a little more exertion matter? There was a table to set and biscuits to mix, and no one else was earning thirty dollars a month to do her chores.

She decided not to look at the foot of her bed, because it was empty. She didn't know Charles Penrose well, but she was certain he would do what he said for Plato, then search every inch of those half-finished rooms down each hall on the first floor with extra-strong boards and longer nails to keep out bears seeking warmth for the winter ahead.

Ellen Found

Ellen groaned and slid out of bed, going to her knees because she had no strength. This would never do. She hauled herself up and sat on her bed until the room stopped whirling. Through grit she didn't know she possessed, she pulled on a petticoat and her best old dress, not wishing to wear the remaining checked shirtwaist and brown skirt and stain it with her blood.

Reaching up to brush her hair was more than she could manage, so she smoothed the ends down with her fingers and tied a shoestring around it. She opened the door and stared into the kitchen, where Mrs. Quincy was making biscuits. A glance beyond into the dining room showed the usual tablecloths on two tables and bowls and spoons, everything in place.

Charles Penrose brought out the coffee mugs and set them around as she watched. He smiled at her. "Mrs. Quincy doesn't trust me with biscuits, and she figured I wouldn't harm anything if I set the tables." He nodded toward two other men. "I have help."

As she leaned against the kitchen door, he came around the table and put an arm around her waist, guiding her to a table. "Mrs. Quincy told me that you wouldn't lie still. I didn't think you would either, but you can sit down and watch us this morning."

Knowing better than to spar with someone whom she didn't think would appreciate an argument, Ellen did as he said. She gasped when she heard a scraping sound from the lobby, and his hand went to her good shoulder. "No fears! They're setting up the hydraulic lift closer to the fireplace to finish the roof." His voice turned serious, hard, even. "Right now we're going through all the rooms. When we find where this bear came in, we'll batten it down and nail the door shut until spring."

"Where . . ." She couldn't say his name.

"You know that little overhang of windows by the kitchen's back door? It was a great place, secluded too, because we know Plato. He won't be crowded there."

She nodded.

"I put Gwen's wool square in my box like you wanted, and I wrapped him in another towel." He took a deep breath. "I did one thing more. I wanted to pet him just once, and I did."

He seemed to gather himself together,

Ellen Found

doing his own reliving of last night's terror. "Gwen told me to tell you not to worry. He'll be warm."

Ellen covered her face with her hands until the moment passed. "Where is Gwen? You shouldn't leave her alone."

"I didn't. Corporal Reeves is in my room. I'll bring Gwen here when she wakes up." He gave her that appraising look she was already familiar with. "We would all feel better if you would lie down."

"That wouldn't earn me my thirty dollars a month," she replied, touched at his concern.

The appraising look turned into something more intense. She felt the warmth of his hand on her shoulder. "You have gone above and beyond earning your thirty dollars this month," he assured her. "I can never put a price on what you did last night."

"I would do it again."

"I know you would." Over her protest—a feeble one—he picked her up and carried her into her room, setting her down on her bed. He looked around and found her hairbrush. He brushed her hair, gentle strokes that soothed her more than anything else possibly could. How did he know?

He seemed to sense her question. "When Clare became agitated about something or other, this always seemed to help." He said it apologetically.

"It does," she said. "No one's ever done this, but it does."

Her eyes closed as she felt herself relax, well aware that in her short lifetime of constantly doing for others, someone—out of kindness or gratitude for his daughter's life, or maybe even because he missed doing this for his wife—was doing something solely for her.

In a few minutes she heard the carpenters, mechanics, and men who fed the hungry generators troop inside for breakfast. She tried to move, to do her job.

"No," Charles said softly. He tied her neat hair back with the shoestring, swung her feet onto the bed, removed her shoes, and covered her with a blanket. "Sleep now."

Before she opened her eyes later, she sensed the presence of someone in the room.

*E*llen Found

For a moment, she hoped it was Charles Penrose.

Mrs. Quincy sat there with a dress across her lap. She stroked the fabric gently, smoothing out wrinkles, and brushing away some speck that Ellen couldn't see. She patted the dress as if someone wore it, then looked up. "Here."

Ellen raised herself on her good arm. Mrs. Quincy helped her sit up, then draped the dress across Ellen's lap. "I took in the hem, so it should fit. She was taller."

Ellen admired the pretty thing, with eyelet lace at the sleeves and a ruffle around the bottom. It was a dress from an earlier time, but not so distant that she hadn't mooned over something like it in a Monkey Ward catalog. "Where did . . ."

"I had a daughter once," the cook said, then left the room quietly.

Ellen stared after her, then touched the dress. *What if I get it dirty working in a kitchen?* warred with, *She wants me to have this. She cares.*

Ellen stared at the ceiling as a great realization settled in. *I doubt there is anyone here who has not suffered a loss*, she thought. *I doubt I am the only child of dubious parentage here. Others are poor, too. Mr. Penrose's wife is dead. One-Eyed Wilson has only one eye, for goodness' sake.*

She thought about Plato, dead after a heroic attempt to protect her, because that's what friends did. She lay there and took a quiet census in her heart.

Corporal Reeves shot the bear. One-Eyed Wilson stitched her shoulder together. Gwen gave Plato a wool square. Mrs. Quincy hemmed her daughter's dress for her. Charles Penrose brushed her hair.

She closed her eyes, thinking through the fear, the pain, the sorrow, and dared to imagine that maybe, just maybe, she had more friends than she knew. What to do with this startling revelation?

I must be a friend, she told herself. *It begins now.*

Ten

Dear Journal, remind me not to think only men are brave and stalwart. I am in debt forever to someone more brave and stalwart than whole armies.

SHE FELT WELL enough after an afternoon nap to put on Mrs. Quincy's gift to her, and it fit. Her shoulder ached, but she could bear the pain. She touched her hair that Charles had brushed so thoroughly. It needed nothing.

Mrs. Quincy was opening cans of green beans in the kitchen. Her eyes seemed to soften as she looked at Ellen in her daughter's dress. She pulled out a chair beside her.

Ellen sat down carefully, fearing any movement that might add more pain. She thought of her resolve and forged ahead. "What was your daughter's name?"

The motion of the can opener stopped. *Maybe I was wrong*, Ellen thought. But no. "Verity. Her ... her father was a New Englander."

"What a beautiful name."

"Yes. Diphtheria took her."

The cook opened another can, then another. "A year later, typhoid took Mr. Quincy, and I moved West."

Mrs. Quincy rested her hand on Ellen's good shoulder, a light touch. "I'm sorry for your losses," Ellen said. She realized she had not known a kind touch before Charles Penrose and now Mrs. Quincy, unless she chose to count Plato's gentle paw on her wrist last night as he surrendered. She chose kindness.

"It was a hard time," Mrs. Quincy said simply. "Everyone knows hard times."

Ellen understood. Others suffered too, but no one spoke of it. She had waited all her life for her luck to turn, and in a moment without warning, it turned. She bowed her head against the emotion.

Ellen Found

Mrs. Quincy pressed down on her good shoulder. "Are you all right?"

"I am," Ellen said, and she was. "I am. How can I help now?"

"Will you be able to stir the gravy while I mash potatoes?"

She did, and no one went hungry. Ellen's worst moment came when, with an apologetic glance, Mrs. Quincy opened the Majestic oven and one of the stronger men pulled out a large pan of roasted bear. Ellen watched as Corporal Reeves carved it and the carpenters served it. As she cautiously took a bite and then another, she felt only triumph. They were eating *the* bear and it seemed right. Drat that bear, but it tasted good.

"Miss Found!"

Ellen turned at the familiar voice and held out her arms. She stifled her pain as Gwen threw herself into her arms and clung to her. In another moment they were holding each other close as Charles Penrose knelt by her chair and somehow held them both. She stroked the child's hair, murmuring words that weren't words as she realized how much she loved Gwen.

"You'll be here in the morning to help me?" she asked when Gwen burrowed as close as last night under the stairs but without the terror. Ellen fingered her soft hair, which smelled of her father's aftershave. "Mrs. Quincy opened an apple barrel, and we're making pie tomorrow."

"I'll be here," Gwen assured her. She put her hands on Ellen's face, drawing her closer. "I found a silk flower for Plato."

"Will you show me where your father buried him?"

Hand in hand, when all Ellen wanted to do was lie down again, they walked out the back door, where Corporal Reeves stood watch, rifle in hand. He nodded to them.

"Miss Found, I telephoned Major Pitcher," he said. "He is sending down two more privates to stand guard here until the bears are denned up. We'll patrol the inn."

She saw him in her mind, kneeling and taking careful aim in the middle of roars and screaming to shoot a bear and save their lives. She held out her hand and he took it. "Thank you seems inadequate."

Ellen Found

"I wish I had been quicker." He let go of her hand and pointed. "Here he is."

In the light from the kitchen, Ellen saw the small mound under the window overhang, a spot no tourist was likely to notice. Only she would remember he was not a showy cat and required no praise, just a scratch behind the ears and whatever the night's menu happened to be, from salmon bits to green beans cooked in bacon fat. And he had saved two lives.

She admired Gwen's rose and looked closer. "Mr. Penrose put the board there," Corporal Reeves explained. He read out loud, "'Plato, 1903. He had a brave heart and was loved.' Mr. Penrose said there will be a headstone later."

"This will do," she said, her heart full. She looked again. "Gwen, is this your lucky magpie feather?"

The child nodded. "If you hold it right, there are green lights."

"Plato never could catch a bird," Ellen said. She felt a tidal wave of grief. "Thank you, Corporal."

She heard the capable man's shyness, followed by a quiet sort of pride. "That's sergeant now. When I called Major Pitcher, he told me that my overdue promotion came through."

"Congratulations, Sergeant Reeves." She kissed his cheek. "That's from me and Gwen."

He took it in stride with a grin. "If you're going to kiss me," he joked, "maybe you'd better call me Tom."

"That's your name?" she asked.

"No, it's Dan," he said with a straight face, then laughed. "Call me Dan."

"Oh, you!" She laughed and it felt good.

Gwen tugged on his sleeve. When he bent down, she kissed his other cheek.

Charles waited for them in the kitchen. He took Ellen aside. "If I can do anything for you, let me," he said, for her ears only.

"Be my friend," she said impulsively. "I'm a little low on friends now."

"No, you're not," he replied. "Not at all."

Eleven

Christmas soon. The bears are denned up, thank God, and our extra guards have returned to Fort Yellowstone, leaving only Sergeant Reeves, a new corporal, and the two privates. Ellen misses Plato. She and Gwen still hesitate when they enter the dark lobby, but she has lost her wary look. She calls me Charles now, and Sergeant Reeves is Dan. One-Eyed Wilson is Mr. Wilson because she defers to age. She is so pretty.

TO EVERYONE'S RELIEF, real snow came at last, snow that meant bears were hibernating. To Mrs. Quincy's delight, Sergeant Reeves and his men shot three wild turkeys for Thanksgiving.

The magical moment for the lobby came

after Thanksgiving dinner when the massive fireplace, with its four hearths, was lit for the first time. "Rumor is the Childs are coming for Thanksgiving," Charles told her.

The Childs arrived at the inn the day after Thanksgiving, accompanying the freight wagons on skids, a four-day journey as the snow deepened.

"I am impressed," Mrs. Quincy said, when the Childs came into the lobby, laughing and shaking off snow, accompanied by the architect. "I didn't think Mrs. High-and-Mighty would want to spend Thanksgiving away from her French chef."

Ellen listened for bitterness, but she didn't hear it. "I wouldn't think Thanksgiving had too many French pilgrims," she teased.

It was a small joke, but Mrs. Quincy laughed. "There's leftover ground turkey. We can call it *les hashe*."

Les hashe it was, flavorful and accompanied by biscuits smothered in turkey gravy. Ellen heard Mr. Reamer ask Harry Child, "We weren't sure you were coming. How did you manage it?"

Mrs. Child waved away any difficulties.

Ellen Found

"Harry and I climbed into the freight wagon four days ago. Call us stowaways! We hunkered down in a pile of blankets intended for the rooms here."

"We wanted to be here," Mr. Child said simply. "You are all working magic."

"I'm certain your French chef was disappointed he couldn't cook for you," Mrs. Quincy said, her voice perfectly bland.

Was Mrs. Child touched by that same bit of Yellowstone magic that Ellen had been feeling despite everything? How else to credit what happened then? Maybe Ellen didn't really know Mrs. Child, except through her boss's jaundiced view.

"Mrs. Quincy, I was perfectly wrong about a French chef," Adelaide Child said, mincing nary a word. "He left in a huff a month ago when all I did was say I'd like bacon and scrambled eggs for dinner, you know, the way you make them."

Stunned silence. Mrs. Quincy stared at her former employer.

"You should have seen his hissy fit," Mrs. Child told her. "I hear he's working for some copper king in Butte now." She took Mrs.

Quincy's hand. "I was wrong, and I apologize. Would you come back and cook for us?"

"I'll think about it," Mrs. Quincy said after she got her breath. "But now, I do have hash, if you don't mind a little solitary splendor in the dining room."

"That would be delightful," Mrs. Child said. "First, though, I want to sit by the fireplace."

Everyone gathered in the lobby, the warmth of the fire reaching into dark corners. It was Ellen's turn to give Mrs. Quincy a little prod in the doorway to get her moving. "I can't believe my ears," her boss whispered to her. "She wants me back."

Ellen squeezed Mrs. Quincy's hand. "Don't leave us." It sounded bold and brave to Ellen, but she meant it. Her answer was a squeeze back.

Even with the warmth and light, Ellen felt a momentary fear of the bear. To her relief, it was now a catching of breath before taking that first step. Gwen moved closer to her. She put her arm around the child even as Charles did the same. Their hands met and he smiled. "No fears, you two," he admonished gently. "You're

Ellen Found

safe. The bears have gone to bed for the winter." He leaned closer to Ellen, his daughter between them. "You'll feel peaceful someday."

His hand was warm on hers. She nodded, too shy to speak. She thought about him later after everyone admired the fireplace, chatted about what lay ahead, and left the building, the Childs to share the photography studio with Mr. Reamer. The glowing coals from the hearths had winked out, and the massive red door, with its iron straps, was closed but not locked. Everyone's goodnights followed a predictable, bravura appearance by Old Faithful. "It never gets old," Mrs. Child said.

Lying in bed, her feet warm, Ellen contemplated how much of that peace came from Charles Penrose, the quiet, capable carpenter and father to a child becoming such a part of her life. What better time to consider the matter of father and daughter, here in bed with the luxury of time to think.

Aided by Mrs. Quincy a week earlier, Charles had done something that Ellen knew she would never forget, no matter how many years passed. When her shoulder still ached, and she grieved the yawning void left by Plato's death, she went to bed one night to discover a hot water bottle wrapped in a towel between the sheets in precisely the place where Plato used to sleep.

As her feet warmed and her heart softened, she knew the gentle blessing of unexpected kindness. She couldn't recall a time when anyone had been so thoughtful. How kind of Mrs. Quincy.

She told her so that morning, and Mrs. Quincy shook her head, her eyes lively. "I'd love to take credit, Ellen, but that goes to Mr. Penrose. He thought you might find it comforting."

"I do," Ellen replied after a moment of amazement. "Charles Penrose?"

Mrs. Quincy continued to amaze her. "I believe he is looking out for you."

"I think he will always be grateful that I . . . I . . . well, you know, kept his daughter safe." She shivered, the memory too real.

"It's more than that," Mrs. Quincy replied. "More." She clapped her hands and broke the spell, but Ellen sensed no harshness. "Let's get busy! Breakfast isn't going to make itself."

Ellen could have said nothing. Maybe the

Ellen Found

Ellie Found who was raised on sufferance wouldn't have. Things were different now. She waited until after breakfast when the architect gave his instructions for the day's work and Charles Penrose made the assignments, then brought his daughter into the kitchen.

Ellen patted Gwen and gave her a gentle nudge. "Mrs. Quincy needs you to help her carry some Carnation cans from the shelves over there," she said, hoping that Mrs. Quincy would understand she wanted a quiet moment with the tall carpenter.

To her delight, Mrs. Quincy didn't hesitate. "Follow me, Gwen," she said, after a slight raise of her eyebrow that spoke louder than words ever could. Ellen had an ally.

With an ache, Ellen realized that she knew nothing about addressing kindness. She took a deep breath and a chance, the same as when she answered the advertisement a few months ago. "Charles, thank you for the hot water bottle," she said, her hands clasped together to keep them from shaking. "It made me a whole lot less sad."

"Oh, I . . ."

Could it be that Mr. Penrose didn't know

what to say either? Ellen felt herself relax, happy to know she wasn't the only shy person. "You were kind," she told him. "I needed that."

To her delight, he seemed to relax too. He glanced at his daughter, busy with Carnation cans, and came closer, keeping his voice low. "After my wife died"—she saw sudden sadness cross his face—"I did that for myself." He hesitated, then must have understood that since he had gone this far, he might as well forge on. "Clare liked to put her cold feet on my legs."

No matter her inexperience, Ellen knew this was a charged, intimate moment, a contained man's attempt that she understood: Loneliness is worse than almost anything. She spoke quietly to him alone, as if the room were empty. "I didn't feel lonely."

"Mrs. Quincy said she would make sure you had it every night."

"I hope you didn't use your only hot water bottle."

"I have another one. That one's yours now."

Such a memory. Mrs. Quincy had not forgotten the water bottle tonight. "Stay here at

Ellen Found

Old Faithful, Mrs. Quincy," Ellen said softly. "We need you . . . I need you . . . here at the inn. Mrs. Child can wait. Please?"

Besides themselves, Mrs. Child had brought along burlap sacks of onions and carrots, and even celery. The next day Harry Child had Charles's crew unload a heavy cache from Mr. Colfitt, ironworker extraordinaire. Straining and sweating, even in below-zero weather, the freighter hauled in crates of Colfitt's best efforts, including iron bands crafted to Mr. Reamer's specifications to wrap around the inn's stone front desk.

Even more remarkable were the electric lights shaped like candles. Charles held one up, turning it to catch the early-morning sun, at least what there was of it.

"Four crates of these, with more to come," he said. "Our electrician arrives in March to wire this whole building. You'll see these everywhere in the lobby and halls."

"Winking little stars among our lodgepole pines," Ellen said, enchanted. "How does Mr. Reamer do it?"

"He has a vision of what can be."

So do I, Ellen thought much later, warming her toes against the hot water bottle after a long day's work. It was still her more-modest vision of wanting something more, but what? Her life had trained her to expect nothing, so the matter required some thought.

Warm from the water bottle, tired from the work, safe with her door closed, and free finally from an aching shoulder, Ellen closed her eyes. Before she slept, she wondered what Charles was going to do with the little iron fish that she saw Mr. Colfitt hand him. Perhaps he had requested it from Mr. Colfitt for his daughter because Christmas was coming. A fish?

She was still thinking of the pretty thing next morning when she opened the back door of the kitchen that led to the massive bear-proof garbage cans, ready to dump in breakfast scraps.

As always, she looked down at Plato's grave, which lately had become a repository of magpie feathers, a shell or two from someone, even a sardine can that made her smile.

There rested the iron fish.

Twelve

I admire Sergeant Dan Reeves. He's careful with his men, and he is fair, if firm. He is a peerless horseman, something I am not. He's equally adept on skis. We trust his judgment. Lately, though, I wish he could find another diversion besides Ellen Found. How is it that Ellen grows more lovely by the day? For a man of at least a little experience with women, I know nothing.

CHRISTMAS CAME, AND for the first time in Ellen's life it meant something besides serving clam chowder—Mr. Linson's one concession to the holiday—to sad-eyed men who had nowhere else to go except the Mercury Street Café.

She wouldn't have told anyone about that, but for some reason, Sergeant Reeves had instituted a nightly walk among the geysers of the upper basin that fronted the inn. It usually began with a view of Old Faithful from the newly completed second-floor porch, with its overhang of roof that kept off the snow.

Provided the weather cooperated, she bundled up in her shabby coat. It didn't look so bad in the dark. Sergeant Reeves—Dan—knew where to walk safely among the geysers and hot pots, and he kept a firm hand on her arm.

He wasn't a talkative man during the day—what she saw of him and his patrol—but the dark made him voluble. He told her about growing up on a farm in Connecticut, a state so far away that she could barely imagine it. "I wanted something more adventurous, and I joined the army," he said. He had more recently finished a tour of duty in the Philippines, and she learned about the insurrectionist Moros, humidity that did wretched things to wounds, and jungle fevers.

"Do I talk too much?" he asked one night.

She assured him he did not. "No. All I ever knew before Yellowstone was Butte,

Ellen Found

Montana," she said. "I hope you've never been there."

He laughed at that. Nights like this, she found it easy not to think of Butte. Plato was seldom far from her thoughts, but they had mellowed, as Charles Penrose had earlier suggested that they would. "I won't say grief vanishes, but it changes, or so I have discovered," was all Charles said about the matter. She knew he meant more than he could express, and she honored that.

"We won't forget Christmas," Mrs. Quincy said one morning. She said it with considerable finality. "I will requisition a suitable tree. Shouldn't be hard to find one."

It wasn't. Ellen asked Dan Reeves to locate a tree, but not a big one. By the week after Thanksgiving, there it was, modestly resting under the *porte cochère*. Decorations proved to be no problem either, and they came from a surprising source: One-Eyed Wilson, a.k.a. Mr. Fred Wilson. "I've been collecting them for years," he told Mrs. Quincy. "Never had a tree before, but I've been hopeful." And that was all he said as he gave Mrs. Quincy his carefully wrapped box.

Presents. Ellen had eight dollars left from her life savings, but she knew there was money percolating now in a Bozeman bank, thanks to her thirty dollars a month. She knew what to get Gwen, who confided in her one morning as they diced potatoes that her papa wrote in a journal every night before he slept. "I wish I had a journal," she said. "Think what I could write, now that I can write a little."

A search for paper in a room containing items stashed for the inn turned up ledgers and a massive book likely intended for the front desk and registration of visitors, come summer. *I daren't use that*, Ellen told herself and continued her search.

She found plain sheets of thick paper between bed linens, for some reason. Twenty sheets easily folded into forty. She knew Mr. Wilson had thick black thread because he had used it on her shoulder. "I'll do it for Gwen," he said.

She debated whether the paper was useful to the inn, finally assuaging her conscience by leaving a dollar and a note among the sheets. The journal became a thing of beauty, carefully stitched down the middle by Mr. Wilson, with

Gwen's name in elaborate script, Ellen's contribution.

Mrs. Quincy became a fellow conspirator. "If I had yarn, I would knit mittens for Dan and Charles," Ellen told her boss over bread-making. The next morning, hanging on her doorknob was a man's sweater with a note attached. *Unravel this*, she read. *Should be enough for mittens.*

Did she even dare ask Mrs. Quincy if this belonged to her late husband? She dared, or almost did. Her "Is this . . ." was enough for a nod. "I shouldn't," Ellen said and tried to hand it back. Mrs. Quincy pressed it into Ellen's hands. "I have his letters and a stickpin," she said. "Put it to good use."

What about Mrs. Quincy? She could tell the constant racket of saws and hammers in the hotel, plus the power drills, taxed the woman. There were long evenings when the cook stood at the large window in the lobby, staring at the deepening snow beyond the overhang of the porch. Ellen consulted with Mr. Wilson, who spent more and more of his time in the kitchen "helping out," as he put it or "mooching for cookies," as Mrs. Quincy said. No matter. The cook never seemed inclined to shoo him away.

"She needs something to cheer her up," Ellen told him.

Mr. Wilson gave the matter some thought. A week before Christmas, when she was knitting mittens in her room at a furious pace, he knocked, identified himself, stuck his arm in, and held out a carved wren no taller than three inches. "I made this," he told her when she opened the door wider, sounding shy and proud at the same time, not like an older gent of some years and one eye, gone in a mysterious time and place.

"Beautiful." Ellen touched the upturned tail. "Maybe she'll think spring is coming."

"My mother did, when I carved my first wren for her."

Do we all have secret lives? Ellen asked herself, humbled by this one-eyed man who had stitched her back together.

She returned to her room and came back with two dollars. He shook his head. "Between you and me, missy, I wanted to give Vera something. You can give it to her. Maybe tell her I made it, if you want to."

Ellen Found

Vera, is it? Ellen thought, delighted. "I can do that," she told him. Vera.

Ellen's gift to everyone was a cake on Christmas Eve, but not just any cake. This one was four layers of chocolate goodness, chocolate because Gwen confided that her father loved chocolate. All Ellen had was cocoa, also "liberated" from pantry supplies clearly labeled *Not for use before summer.* She put another of her vanishing dollars by the cocoa tin and a note.

In a democratic vein, as in, "All in favor say aye," everyone agreed that the big dinner would be Christmas Eve, whereupon there would be silence and sleeping in on Christmas Day, which Mr. Child, via telegram, had declared would be a day off with pay. "Leftovers will be generous," Mrs. Quincy assured them. "Ellen and I deserve a day off, too."

The banging and drilling and sawing continued through the afternoon as Ellen and Mrs. Quincy cooked, ably assisted by Gwen, who confided to Ellen that she had a tidy stack of one-dollar bills, her salary for helping. "I wish I could spend them somewhere," she told

Ellen after her nap. "I wanted to get Papa a new cravat. He's not very stylish," she added, which made Ellen laugh.

"It'll keep, my dear. Here's a sheet of paper. Draw him what you want to give him."

Gwen flashed her a smile, reminding Ellen how much she looked like her father, who, for some reason, wasn't smiling so much. Maybe Christmas did that to some people. Mrs. Quincy continued to gaze out the window and rub her arms. As for her, Ellen could barely contain herself. Christmas in the Copper King house just meant more work. In the Mercury Street Café, it meant sad people with nowhere to go. This was better.

At six o'clock, all drills and sawing stopped. Someone lit two hearths of the massive fireplace this time, which made Gwen clap her hands. Ellen watched her from the dining room as she sat in one of the new wicker chairs, her feet not touching the floor, chairs intended for grown-up summer visitors. Gwen's fear of the lobby had vanished, but then Gwen had not felt the claw on her shoulder. *Thank goodness for that*, Ellen thought.

Probably against orders—but who was

Ellen Found

there to object?—Ellen and Mrs. Quincy dug around in the kitchen crates and favored the crew with Blue Willow dishes this time. "No one will know," her boss said. She put her hands on her hips. "Besides, they're just rough men."

Ellen smiled to herself, amused that Mrs. Quincy still thought of herself as a woman hardened through tough times. She had seen the way she tucked Gwen in for a nap when Ellen was too busy, or the extra cookies that came Mr. Wilson's way. *Are we all changing?* she asked herself.

Mr. Reamer didn't always join them for dinner, but this was different. There were no railroad financiers to impress on Christmas Eve, only the men and two women and a girl doing the work that would turn this hulk of a building into a magical place. In his quiet way, he stood and tapped on his glass when the wondrous dinner of elk and turkey and mounds of mashed potatoes and chocolate cake was a pleasant memory.

"Thank you for what you are doing," he said simply. "We would probably all rather be somewhere else this holiday, raising a toast with loved ones, but here we are."

Ellen looked around, amazed at the lump in her throat. There was nowhere she would rather be than right here, right now. She glanced at Charles, who was looking at her, and then down at his daughter. There sat Sergeant Reeves with his men. She blushed when he winked.

"I wish you a Merry Christmas, gentlemen," Mr. Reamer continued. He nodded to Ellen, Mrs. Quincy, and Gwen. "And the ladies, of course." He chuckled. "I know it's hard to contemplate right now in this stage of construction, but someday millions of people will pass through these doors. We will be remembered in the wood, the stone, our electric candlesticks"—everyone laughed—"and our rustic hospitality. To quote the inimitable Tiny Tim, 'God bless us, everyone!'"

Everyone applauded. Charles Penrose raised his hand and gave a nod in the architect's direction. "Sir, we have an early Christmas present for you."

He motioned to the architect, then picked

Ellen Found

up Gwen and carried her at the head of his crew into the lobby. Several of the men carrying lanterns led the way. They stopped in front of one of the guest rooms, one with an iron "1" on the door, part of the pile of numbers Mr. Colfitt had sent ahead. He opened the door and gestured.

"Here you are, Mr. Reamer, a portion of the magic. We wanted to complete one room."

"Oh my," Ellen whispered as she took in the iron bedstead and the mattress, two chairs with cushions, a rustic bureau, and a washstand with a cream-colored pitcher and bowl. The curtains at the window, with its many small panes, looked suspiciously like a gathered sheet. Underfoot was a rag rug.

"Just one hundred and thirty-nine rooms to go!" Mr. Wilson said to laughter.

Gradually, the men moved away, chatting in small groups, heading toward their own rustic boardinghouse, destined to be torn down when the project ended, and they moved on to other jobs.

Mr. Reamer cleaned his glasses thoughtfully, carefully, as he did everything. "Thank you for this Christmas surprise, Charles," he said. "It means more than I can say. Bless you all, and good night."

Thirteen

What a paltry present I gave Ellen Found. Maybe I can redeem myself in the spring, if ever I can get to a store. What would be the perfect gift for her?

"STAY A BIT," Ellen said to Charles and Gwen. "I have something for you."

She had never received a present of any kind in her life, but here was One-Eyed—no, Fred Wilson—smiling at her, obviously curious to know how Mrs. Quincy would react to his carving.

Sergeant Reeves started to follow his men, but Ellen told him to wait too, hoping he wouldn't be teased later by this little group he commanded. Not for nothing had she stayed up nearly all night, knitting like fury to finish the mittens.

Charles whispered to Gwen and patted her shoulder, then shrugged on his overcoat and hurried after the two privates Sergeant Reeves sent on ahead. "I'll be right back."

Mrs. Quincy turned her attention to the tree, a modest lodgepole pine that knew better than to compete with the potential majesty of the unfinished lobby. Mr. Wilson's ornaments were positively perfect.

Ellen went to her room for her presents, which now seemed so paltry. What was she thinking? She picked up the presents wrapped in brown paper, the only thing available, and set them beside the tree.

Mrs. Quincy already sat in the step-down area around the fireplace, Mr. Wilson beside her. Ellen noticed for the first time that he must have stood closer to his razor than usual, and she didn't know he owned a white shirt.

Here she was, wearing the brown skirt and gingham shirtwaist because this was a special occasion. The contrast couldn't have been greater between tonight's feast and last year's hurried cheese and crackers and the sad men with nowhere to go on Christmas Eve except the Mercury Street Café. She was well-fed and wearing a new dress. Her shoulder barely pained her. If there was never to be a better Christmas Eve than this one, it was enough.

"I think my father's been hiding a book for me," Gwen whispered to Ellen when she joined her by the fireplace.

"I hope it's one you'll let me read to you," Ellen said.

Sure enough, Charles returned with a book-shaped present, also done up in brown paper. Sergeant Reeves sat beside her. "I wanted to get you something," he whispered, his eyes on Charles, "but I couldn't even get past Fort Yellowstone this winter, let alone Gardiner. Maybe a bouquet of sagebrush when the snow melts a little?" All she could do was blush and smile. It was more than enough.

Charles added a log to the fireplace and joined them after dropping his present by the tree. "It's so little," he murmured.

"Books are everything," she reminded him.

This event was her idea, so everyone

looked at her. Ellen stood up, heart in her mouth, as she realized *she* had engineered this, from the tree on down. She glanced at Mr. Wilson, her fellow conspirator, who nodded his encouragement.

Everyone also knew her circumstances. She took a deep breath. "I never had a tree, and I never had a Christmas Eve dinner." She smiled at Gwen, on sure ground now with the friendly child who had first sat with her on the train, and whose life she'd saved. Her heart swelled with an odd feeling of commitment or camaraderie. Maybe it was love. She didn't know, but it was Christmas Eve in a wonderful place she could never have imagined only months ago.

"Gwen told me that her father writes in a journal," she said. She handed her present to the wide-eyed child. "Mr. Wilson and I did this, Gwen. Merry Christmas."

With the studied efficiency of someone who had opened many a present, Gwen carefully removed the yarn bow made from the final row of yarn on that old sweater from Mrs. Quincy. Gwen opened the journal and turned the blank pages Mr. Wilson had stitched together. "Papa, we can both write each night, can't we?"

"We can, my dearest," he said, with a long look at Ellen that made her stomach settle lower in her lap. He handed Gwen his present, which proved to be *The Tailor of Gloucester*. She pointed to the word. "Gloucester," Charles said. "I know how you liked *Peter Rabbit*. This is by the same author."

She hugged her father and Ellen, and after a moment's shyness, Mr. Wilson, who rubbed his remaining eye and mumbled something about dust.

Such a moment. Ellen had never seen presents exchanged, and she knew she would remember the good feeling forever. But here was Mr. Wilson nudging her. "No, I think you should present it to her," she said, handing him the package. "I knew Mr. Wilson likes to carve," she said to them all, "and I asked him for something for you that reminded him of spring, Mrs. Quincy."

Her boss gasped and shook her head, but Mr. Wilson wasn't about to back down, now that he had the courage. Vera Quincy's fingers shook as she unwrapped the carved wren, that perky little bird that was long gone to warmer climates as winter reigned.

"We . . . we both wanted to cheer you a little," Ellen said.

Mrs. Quincy dabbed at her eyes but made no comment about dust. "I'll set this wren where we can all see it. Spring is still a long way off."

Ellen picked up the two remaining packages, handing the first one to Dan Reeves. She decided in that moment and forever after to say what she meant. "This is from Gwen and me. Thank you for having a steady aim that . . . that night."

"Anyone with a rifle would have done what I did," he said.

"But you were there, and you did it." She touched her heart. "I will never forget."

He swallowed several times, then took out the mittens and put them on. "I have regulation gloves, but it can get pretty cold out in the weather," he said simply. "This'll help." He kissed her cheek.

She handed the other package to Charles. "Your gloves have gotten a bit raggedy from all those heated nails," she told him. She wanted to laugh, but the mood in the room was strange to her. "You have one hundred and thirty-nine other rooms to finish down cold corridors."

Everyone laughed, maybe willing to forget frigid days for a few hours. Mrs. Quincy hurried into the kitchen and came back with more cookies. "Divide these," she ordered. "Ellen and I will bake more tomorrow for the rest of the crew. Thank you all, and good night."

"One moment."

From her apron Ellen took the envelope Mr. Reamer had handed her earlier and gave it to Mrs. Quincy. "This is from Mrs. Child to you, Mrs. Quincy."

"Oh no!"

"Go on," she coaxed. "Look what she wrote on the back."

Mrs. Quincy turned over the letter slowly, as if fearing what she would see. "A Christmas surprise?"

Mrs. Child isn't unkind, Ellen thought. "It can't be that bad."

"If I must." Mrs. Quincy opened the envelope and read the letter. Her expression changed. "I never in my life . . ." Mrs. Quincy sat down. "She's officially offering me my job back. I guess she *was* right about the French chef."

The others applauded, but no one looked happy, especially Mr. Wilson. Mrs. Quincy fanned herself with the letter. "I have until spring to think about it. I might stay."

Ellen glanced at Mr. Wilson. *This could be an interesting spring*, she thought.

"It's been a good day," Mr. Wilson said as he and Charles doused the fires. Sergeant Reeves gave Ellen a small salute. As he left the lobby, she heard him whistling "Good King Wenceslas."

She took Mr. Wilson's arm and escorted him to the door. "Thank you, Mr. Wilson. The wren was perfect."

"Thank *you*. I've been wanting to do something nice for her." He chuckled. "Guess I needed a nudge."

She waved goodnight to the Penroses and followed Mrs. Quincy into the kitchen. The dishes were done, and plates were ready for tomorrow's pancakes and bacon, a rare treat, but it was Christmas Day, after all. There were

ℰllen Found

ample leftovers for the day, so it would be like a little kitchen vacation for them.

Mrs. Quincy hugged her and went to her room, leaving Ellen to douse the lights. Ellen left one lantern burning and went to the back door, happy for a small moment with Plato. She looked down at the snow-covered mound of the bravest cat in the universe.

"Ellen, do you have a moment?"

Startled, she turned around to see Charles Penrose standing inside the kitchen. She hurried inside, hoping he wouldn't think her a fool for mooning over Plato.

"I have something for you. I wanted you to have this without an audience." He held out an envelope.

A present. Her name in firm lettering. *I will keep this envelope forever*, she thought. She opened it. Seeds. Charles came closer.

"Every autumn, Clare shook seeds out of her summer flowers," he said, his voice low, even with no one else around to hear. "She never was able to plant these, and I've hung on to them for two years."

"I can't . . ." she began.

He raised his hand. "You can, please.

When spring comes, plant them on Plato's grave. Goodnight, and Happy Christmas."

Ellen wished she could tell him that no one had ever done a nicer thing for her, but he would probably scoff at that. "I will save some of the seeds. You and Gwen can plant them later, somewhere else."

"If you'd like." He drew her close for a surprising moment. "Thank you again for my daughter's life. Words can be inadequate, even for a Cornishman."

"It's just that . . ." How to explain this? "I wish I could have done better for Plato."

"If we could delve into the feline mind, I think Plato would say you did very well by him."

"I wish I felt worthy of that much devotion," she admitted, surprising herself. "Who am I, after all? My mother—"

"You never knew her."

"But she was—"

"And you are you," he said firmly. "I have something to say."

She wondered at this quiet, capable man who usually kept his thoughts to himself. Why was he going to this trouble for her?

Ellen Found

"When I was eight, my father came out of the Dalcoath tin mine and said we were going to America," he told her. "He never said what happened in the pit to cause such a decision. We came to America and managed well enough."

"You had family. I have no one," she reminded him. "No one now."

"Are you so certain? My father worked with wood. He taught me everything I know and use today. The way I see it, you are your own teacher. Never discount that."

"I have nothing!" she said, trying to remind him, the stubborn man.

He put his finger to her lips. "Most of us require teachers. You taught yourself kindness and bravery. You taught *yourself*. Think on that."

She stayed a long time in the kitchen, holding the envelope to her cheek.

Fourteen

Did I say too much? Was I too impulsive? We're working too hard, but we must. The electricians have created their magic. Ellen Found is also lovely by electric light. The plumbers are going to spoil us soon with indoor plumbing. I remember how nice it was when Clare scrubbed my back in the tub. I miss that. I miss a lot of things.

EVERYONE BUCKLED DOWN even more after Christmas. January saw the welcome addition of Mr. Colfitt, who set up his temporary forge and shop practically by the inn's back door. He also brought with him more electric candlesticks and an amazing five-foot iron clock that Mr. Reamer had designed for the fireplace.

Ellen Found

After surveying the situation and muttering to himself, Mr. Colfitt forged an iron ladder-bridge from the second floor landing out to the massive fireplace. Ellen watched two brave souls inch across, affix the massive clock to the fireplace, and set it ticking. "Someone has to wind that monster once a week," Charles said over coffee the next morning. "Not me!"

Charles made no mention of their Christmas Eve conversation. He didn't avoid her, but he remained his usual, quiet self. Ellen considered the matter as she grieved for Plato, wishing she could have . . . what? "He chose to stay with me for two years," she told herself late one night. "He didn't have to, but he did. I should let this rest." She slept better after that.

Next came the inn's electrification. Mr. Reamer called them artificers, those two fellows from Bozeman who, with Mr. Colfitt, wired the electric candlesticks throughout the lobby, down halls, and into guest rooms, where the carpenters hammered and sawed.

For a quiet man, Mr. Reamer had a dramatic flair. At nightfall in mid-February he announced over dinner that now was the time. "Gentlemen and ladies, join me in the lobby."

Everyone watched as the architect and his electricians moved to the wall behind the front desk and Mr. Reamer flicked the switch. Each electric candlestick seemed to light itself by magic. Gwen clapped her hands.

Ellen stared in wonder. She looked around at tired faces that didn't seem so tired. Maybe it was a trick of light after all these months of gloom and snow. She decided it was pride in the work, a commitment to a unique building in the wilderness and its pinpoints of light.

These electric beauties couldn't flicker like ordinary candles. Their steady light shone on lodgepole pine walls and oddly shaped, lacquered branches twisting under the handrails. She took a good look at the small landing near the pinnacle of the roof where Mr. Reamer said a string quartet would perform during dinner and dancing. The crew already called it the Crow's Nest.

She knew Plato would have enjoyed such a perch. Lately, she could think calmly of him, sorrow replaced by good memories and gratitude without relentless grief. Maybe Charles Penrose was right.

Ellen Found

"There is nothing like this anywhere," the architect said, recalling her to the moment. "June first, my friends," he told them. "We are making history."

Plumbers came the next week, bundled up in freight wagons on skids. With electric lights, the carpenters worked even later hours on room after room. Ellen saw the toll it took on Charles Penrose, the man she enjoyed seeing every morning for coffee. Now he carried a drowsy Gwen into Ellen's room, where she patted Ellen's pillow and returned to slumber.

"Your face is too thin," she told Charles one morning. Electric lights made it harder to hide exhaustion. "Being in charge can't be easy."

He smiled at that, which helped her heart, that odd organ that lately seemed to govern more than her wary brain. Why else did she want to tuck his muffler tighter into his overcoat?

"I'll survive," he assured her one morning. "Sit down. You're too busy. Just sit with me."

She sat, hoping he would say more. She pushed forward a plate of Mrs. Quincy's doughnuts. He took one, nodding his appreciation. *Say more*, she thought, then thought the impossible: *I want to know you better.*

Maybe he was feeling expansive. Maybe more at ease. Maybe it was the doughnuts. He leaned back in his chair. "Clare would do that—bustle about until I grabbed her and sat her down. We didn't usually say much. It was enough to just . . . just . . . *be*. Try it."

One morning he asked her about Mrs. Quincy. "She seems different these days," he said, then gave her a broad smile, as he used to before the work began to wear him out. "May I give the credit to Fred Wilson?"

She nodded, pleased that'd he noticed. "She doesn't stare out the window so much," Ellen confided. "She makes ever so many doughnuts. She won't admit they're for Mr. Wilson, but I know better."

Then came the morning when his guard must have been down. "The fellows tell me that Sergeant Reeves always seems to find something to do here when he isn't on patrol."

"He does," she agreed, wondering what to make of this widower, this tentative man.

Ellen Found

"He's a good fellow with a promising future in the army," he said. She listened for animosity but heard only words carefully chosen.

"He has plans," she said, choosing carefully too, because she liked Dan Reeves.

"Do his plans include you?" he blurted out another morning.

"He hasn't said so," she replied, wanting to shake him a little, or maybe a lot, because she realized that somewhere between the envelope of seeds and iron fish, something had happened to her. And so she sat with the tentative widower who touched her mind and heart.

She taught Gwen to make biscuits, and how to French braid her own hair. "After all, when this project is done, you'll be moving to another place with your father," she said, which broke her heart in ways she hadn't reckoned on.

Mr. Reamer asked her and Mrs. Quincy to increase their chores to include sweeping out the finished rooms and wiping them down. "That last freight sled brought in iron bedsteads and bedding," he told her. "The chairs and bureaus are here too. Time to furnish the rooms."

Mrs. Quincy asked her to work with Gwen. "I work better alone," she assured Ellen, who wasn't even slightly fooled. Mr. Wilson always managed to show up to sweep and mop too. She heard them laughing together down the hall and felt a twinge of envy.

"Does he like Mrs. Quincy?" Gwen asked her once when it was almost warm enough to open a window. "She doesn't seem to grumble as much."

Ellen kissed the top of her head.

"I am observant," Gwen told her. She plumped herself down on a bed. "Papa doesn't write so much in his journal. He stares at the pages, then shakes his head and closes it."

"Do you write in yours?" Ellen asked, powerfully wanting to have a look at Charles Penrose's journal.

"Aye." She leaned closer. "Papa is hoping to get another assignment here in the park. A place called Lake. Are you staying here?"

"I hope to."

"Come with us to Lake," Gwen said. "You'll be too far away here. I ... I asked my father if you could come with us."

Ellen heard the urgency and sat down

Ellen Found

beside the little one. She held her close. "What did he say?"

"He kissed my cheek like you kissed my head. I am getting nowhere with him!"

I know the feeling, Ellen thought.

The days began to lengthen as snow moved from endless powder to wet, heavy flakes that signaled a change of season. Already some of the workers had left for other jobs. The only thing that made her happy about that were their bashful thanks to her for good food, something she never heard at the Mercury Street Café.

Sergeant Reeves came by more often after supper. The exhaustion of cold patrols on skis and frustrating searches for poachers who robbed Yellowstone for their own enrichment had left its mark. As worn down as he was, she knew he would show up after dishes were done to walk with her in the geyser basin.

The snow never stayed long there, vanquished by the everlasting warmth of fumaroles, hot pots, and geysers. As impressive as they were, none of them rivaled nearby Old Faithful, which showed itself at a regular fifty-five minutes, but life, she knew, was seldom spectacular.

"Think of the tourists coming in June," Dan said one evening as they strolled. "They'll ooh and aah, but for my money, I like this basin."

They paused to watch Old Faithful erupt. Who wouldn't? As they watched, she told the sergeant her plan. "I've applied for a position as front desk clerk here."

"You'll get it." He turned to her. "You're the kind of pretty girl Mr. Child wants to see in his hotel."

"Thanks, Dan." Goodness. Better make a joke. "I should have put my hair up months ago," she told him. "Every girl likes a compliment."

"It's more than that, Ellen," he said, more serious now than she had seen him. "You have kind eyes and a good heart, and it shows."

He had kissed her before on the cheek, but this was different. This was a serious kiss on the lips, her first ever. "Been wanting to do that," he whispered when his lips still nearly touched hers.

She strolled with him, shy and pleased.

Ellen Found

She knew Dan Reeves was a good man with honorable intentions, the sort of man she could never have found anywhere near the Mercury Street Café. In her short lifetime of wanting little because she had next to nothing, she had wanted more. That wanting had brought her to Old Faithful Inn.

To her chagrin, she still wanted more.

Fifteen

What do I do? I'm thirty-two years old, and I'm thinking like twenty again. I'll be ~~damned~~ darned if the sap rises in places besides pine trees.

AFTER ONLY A few blocks, Charles knew Ellen was right about Butte. It was a no-account town with more bars and brothels than churches. He gave Butte the benefit of the doubt at the depot. He had been around enough depots to know that things looked better after a few blocks. Not in Butte.

He was only supposed to go to Bozeman to inspect and purchase a new power saw, except that the salesman didn't know his Bozemans from his Buttes. "You'll find what

Ellen Found

you want in Butte," he said with no apology. Ah well. The day was warm, and he was amenable to a little longer with nothing to do, a rare novelty. A telegram to Mr. Reamer easily explained a few more days away.

More than that, he wanted to think. He'd said nothing to Ellen—it was hardly his business—but he had seen Sergeant Reeves kiss her at the upper basin last week.

At least it wasn't a long kiss. Maybe a business trip with time on the train would give him the courage to admit to himself what he had known for some time: he was in love with Ellen Found.

He knew he could rationalize the powerful emotion that played merry hell with his peace of mind. Gwen needed a mother. A man was entitled to another wife to make his way easy in life.

It was time he admitted to himself that Gwen had not once entered into his desire to marry Ellen. He wanted Ellen as much as he had wanted Clare Hayden, and for the same reasons. He missed the pleasure of married life, from the simplicity of sharing a pillow and talking about life plans, to the complexity of loving a woman because he had urges that weren't going away.

He smiled to himself as he walked along streets dirty with black snow found in mining towns like Butte. He was thirty-two years old but as frisky as a colt.

He stopped in front of a shop window to stare at himself in the reflection. He knew he was a handsome man. Clare used to get tight-lipped when women stared at him and flirted. He pleaded innocence because he didn't care as long as Clare found him attractive. He could easily have enjoyed a lifetime with her, but fate had shuffled their cards.

Now he found a promising future in Yellowstone. A recent letter from Harry Child stated there was work to be done finishing the remodel at Lake Hotel as soon as Old Faithful Inn was completed, and was he interested? Aye he was. And could it also involve Ellen?

What prevented him from being the man kissing Ellen? Did he need some cosmic approval to marry again, have more children with likely an excellent mother, and grow old with someone besides his first love?

He stared at his reflection, which had

Ellen Found

turned glum and stupidly pathetic. "I want a wife," he told his wavy image. "It's no crime."

He'd started contemplating remarriage a year ago when the raw hurt of Clare's lingering death from a failing heart had turned to a dull ache and then to tender memories of a woman he loved who died too soon. He decided he should look for a wife like the one he had lost.

Then why Ellen? From her dark looks and olive skin, she possessed none of Clare's rosy complexion or her majestic height and truly elegant features. Ellen was small and energetic, with wonderful brown eyes and black hair. With that energy came a quiet nature at odds with the fervor of her labors. Perhaps he could trace that to a child trained from youth to be seen and not heard, a child of low origin that was somehow her fault. Ellen was a person on her own from youth.

She was also the bravest person Charles knew, someone who did not lose her head in a crisis, someone ready to sacrifice herself for another. He doubted he had that much courage and prayed it would never be tested. He could tell Ellen loved his daughter. Did Ellen love him too?

Enough of this; he was here on business. Charles purchased the power saw to replace the saw and bits worn out with chewing into lodgepole pine. He handed over the cheque from Harry Child and received a receipt and guarantee that it would arrive in Gardiner, Montana, in two weeks. Done.

He didn't want to stay another moment in Butte. He already had a ticket for tomorrow's first train to Bozeman, but that was tomorrow. *I wonder* ... he thought, then turned back to the clerk. "Where is the Mercury Street Café?" he asked.

The clerk stared at him, maybe seeing a capable man wearing a good overcoat, and wondering why on earth ... "It's not a place for gents like you," the clerk said tentatively.

"I know someone who worked there, and I was wondering ..." Charles saw the smirk. "No, not *that* sort of person."

"I'm relieved to say it burned to the ground two weeks ago."

Insufferable prig, Charles thought, then, "*Really?* I'd still like to see it."

The clerk pointed. "Two blocks that way,

then three more north." He stifled a laugh. "Nasty place. Glad it's gone."

Two blocks took Charles into an even worse part of town, where women wearing nothing but wrappers and smiles leaned out windows. One whistled at him and made a vulgar comment about the swing to his walk. He blushed at the unwanted attention. Clare had mentioned that swing herself, but not while leaning out a window.

There it was, a blackened heap giving new meaning to the word "eyesore." He breathed in the stink of burned wood and old grease that had probably been trapped in drains since the town's founding. Someone had hung a sign, "Too bad, so sad."

A merchant stood in the doorway across the street; Charles joined him. "I used to know someone who worked here," he said, wondering if he should admit that he knew *anyone* associated with the café. "A kind woman with a mean cat."

"Meanest cat that ever lived," the man said with a laugh. "I hear she snuck out at midnight a few months ago, cat and all."

"She did. You knew her?"

"She bought soap and tooth powder from me. She asked to use my address as a return address for a job she wanted. She got the job?"

"A good job," Charles said, then nodded at the eyesore. "What happened?"

"Ol' Linson had a cook who smoked. Near as anyone can figure, she dropped ashes on a pile of newspapers, and whoosh!"

"That bad?"

"That bad. The old rip flicked her final ash. Linson left town the next morning, and good riddance." He paused, then peddled back a bit. "Hopefully you're not related to him."

"Not I."

"Good." His face took on a wistful expression. "That little lady who got away . . . she was a pretty thing with kind eyes, but oh, that cat."

Charles almost told the merchant how Plato the demon cat saved his daughter's life and the life of that pretty thing, but that meant more questions. He nodded his goodbye and strolled down the street.

Making sure he wasn't being watched, he found his way to the alley. The burn smell was even stronger, along with alley odors best left

Ellen Found

unidentified. He paused before a door hanging off its hinges. In his mind's eye, he saw a woman of courage and determination living there, sharing her skimpy meals with a cat.

He looked inside to see a precarious ceiling sagging and a rotting floor. The bed was no more than a cot, and there was a three-legged table and one stool. Pages from magazines were still tacked to the walls, photographs of mountains and streams, and a lady in a frilly dress. With a pang, he wondered if Ellen had tacked the picture there, her homage to a mother she never knew, a lady of the line, but her mother despite all.

"Family's what you make it, dear lady," he said.

Where now? He didn't want to pass those ogling harpies again, so he walked up the alley. He slowed, knowing he was being followed. He tightened his grip on his carpetbag and turned around.

It was a cat. No, a kitten, ambling along, maybe following him, maybe not. Who knew with cats? He watched, amused, as it pounced on a leaf, tried to eat it, then found a prize. He looked closer as the kitten wriggled its backside, then pounced on a cricket that had somehow survived into winter. It ate with some relish, then looked around for more.

"Tight times, little buddy," Charles said softly.

He had always been a careful man, measuring twice before cutting once, taking good care of his wife and daughter, and then his daughter. He kept his saws sharp, and he hammered nails straight and true. He left little to chance, because that was how buildings fell down and chairs collapsed.

In an impulsive gesture he could only credit to a longing to make a pretty lady happy again, he knelt. "How about you come with me ... uh ... Socrates?"

Without a hiss or a backward glance, the little morsel made no objection when Charles deposited it in his overcoat pocket. To his surprise, he felt an outsized purr against his hip. He stopped at an emporium near what looked like the least-scabrous hotel in town and bought several cans of Carnation, a can opener, and some sardine tins.

"You're changing residence, Socrates," he said the next morning as the kitten, its belly

Ellen Found

full of milk and sardines, nestled in his carpetbag.

Careful as always, he telegraphed ahead, so there was a freight wagon held for him at Fort Yellowstone, full of crates and furniture labeled *Old Faithful Inn*. He looked around, amazed at what a few days away could do. The great melt was on. The wagon had wheels again and not skids.

"Getting ready to open that hotel?" the driver said as he joined him on the wagon seat, carpetbag at his feet, Socrates inside.

"We are. Rooms are almost done. And you're hauling more furniture."

As they rode by mounds of melting slush, Ellen Found occupied his mind. He reconsidered. His heart was occupied. The obstacle was Sergeant Reeves. *We shall see*, he thought. *I've courted a woman before*.

They were almost through scary Golden Gate, that maze of curves and hoodoos where the road cantilevered out over the Gardner River far below, when the driver glanced over his shoulder. "Uh oh," he said, then something not repeated in polite company.

Uneasy, Charles looked back just as a

sudden gust of blizzard wind roared down his overcoat collar, followed by icy pellets. The sky vanished in a swirl of snow.

"I can't see ahead," the driver said. Charles heard the panic in his voice. "Why'd this happen right here? I daren't move. Didja bring any food?"

Sixteen

I am afrad. It's a blitzerd. Did I spell that right? I thot the snow was gone. We all did. My father has been gon to long. Ellen wipes my tears when I cry. She cries latter, when no one noes. When Da comes hom, I will tell him I let Ellen reed his jurnal. I wunder if he will be angree.

ON THE FIRST morning she didn't wear her coat, Ellen knew it was time to plant Charles Penrose's gift of seeds on Plato's grave.

A look around suggested the coming of summer. Soon leaves would bud out, revealing that impossible green heralding spring and early summer. Already the chipmunks chattered at her.

The snow was gone from Plato's mound. Humming to herself, she made four little furrows and carefully spaced the seeds, leaving a few seeds in the envelope in case Charles wanted some after all.

"Lots of critters around soon," she told Plato as she patted his grave. "I doubt you could have caught them, but I know you would have tried."

She stood there, hands together, then turned toward the northwest as a sudden gust of what felt suspiciously like winter ruffled her skirt and showed off her ankles. The next blast brought wet and heavy snow with it. She ran inside and slammed the door behind her.

For three days snow fell without pause, the wind blowing it into monstrous drifts. The ropes between the inn and temporary housing went up again. Men shrugged and muttered about, "Mother Nature's dirty tricks," and, "That's Wyoming for you."

Temperatures dropped to negative numbers. Ellen didn't think Sergeant Reeves and his men would leave the confines of their quarters, but he came through the storm that fourth day, looking grim about the mouth. While she made breakfast biscuits and worried, he handed her a message.

Ellen Found

"Before the telephone line went down, this came from headquarters. Mr. Penrose sent it to the YP transport barn five days ago. I don't know, Ellen."

She made herself read it. "'Arrived Bozeman. Tell freight wagon to wait for me. C. Penrose.'" She looked at Dan. "He's probably still at Fort Yellowstone, then?" she asked, trying to sound casual.

Dan shook his head. "Not according to the adjutant who read this to me. They started out three days ago. He said Mr. Penrose was eager to get back here. 'I have something for Miss Found,' he told the adjutant."

She turned away and banged the biscuit dough around. He put his hand on her shoulder, but she shook it off. "I am fine," she said through clenched teeth. He left without a word.

She was far from fine. She thought of the many places where a misstep of a horse or wrong command from the driver could send team and wagon down into disaster. *Please let them be past Golden Gate*, she prayed. *That's the worst spot.*

The men ate breakfast with their usual

relish. As she refilled coffee cups, she heard conversations about summer jobs and work for the lucky ones hired to build a YP transportation barn in Gardiner, designed by Mr. Reamer as well. With an ache, she knew the transportation company was missing a wagon and driver. Better not to think about it.

How did such things happen? By the noon meal, everyone knew about the missing wagon, along with a driver and Mr. Penrose. Gwen heard it. She ran to Ellen as she sliced meat and cheese. She clung to Ellen's dress.

"I'll finish up here," Mrs. Quincy said. "Take her to your room."

Ellen picked up the child and retreated to her sanctuary, bright now with the addition of a rug like the ones in the guest rooms. Only yesterday, the carpenters applauded when Mr. Wilson proudly attached the iron numbers 1-1-0 to a door. She heard him say, "Wait'll Mr. Penrose sees this! He was hoping we'd finish off 105 before he came back."

She held Gwen and crooned to her, telling her not to worry, that her father was a careful man and he would show up soon. When Gwen slept, it was Ellen's turn to weep.

𝓔llen Found

The snow stopped a day later, but the wind blew even harder from the north and west, testing the windows, trying to get inside. "We built this inn to last," Mr. Wilson told her that night after a silent dinner. He assured her that carpenters and soldiers would turn into road crews and start out from both ends when the wind stopped.

Gwen worked quietly beside her, not leaving her side. When the dishes were done, she took Gwen's hand and walked her into the wonderful lobby. Someone had lit a fire in one of the hearths. She looked up to see the iron clock Mr. Colfitt had fashioned, ticking away the hours, untroubled by grief or fear, marking time as they waited and worried.

Mr. Reamer left the electric candlesticks on. They sent their cheery glow into the darkness as if to say, "We're here. We're your beacon." Ellen sat on a wicker chair in the stepdown area before the fireplace, Gwen nestled in her lap.

"Could you do something for me?" Gwen asked Mr. Wilson when he and Mrs. Quincy joined them, hand in hand.

"Anything," the one-eyed carpenter said.

"Could you please get my da's journal from our house?" Gwen was a polite child. "And ... and ... could you get his flannel nightshirt? I like the way it smells."

Mrs. Quincy turned her head away. Ellen stared at the flames.

Mr. Wilson returned, snow-covered, with the journal tucked inside his overcoat, along with the nightshirt. With a sigh that made Ellen bite her lip, Gwen tucked the flannel shirt close and handed Ellen the journal. "Maybe you could read some of this to me."

Ellen nodded. "I will," she said softly, "but not right now. Let's cuddle instead."

"I understand," the child said, sounding astoundingly mature.

They cuddled all night, Gwen in tears until she wore herself out, her cheek resting on Charles's nightshirt. When Ellen was certain she slept, she took the journal and a blanket to her armchair and started to read.

Much of the journal was a laconic affair. Some entries only mentioned difficulties in getting quality lumber in Cheyenne, where they lived at the time. Of Gwen's birth he wrote, *Is it possible to love someone more?*

Ellen Found

And to love someone you've only just met? I am proof of that. My girls.

The journal grew even more spare during the time she supposed that Clare Penrose was dying. The hardest entry was the most brief: *What will I do?*

Ellen understood. *What will I do?* she wanted to ask the universe at large. There had certainly been no amazing pronouncements, no fervent declarations of anything between the two of them. She had no claim on Charles Penrose beyond that one long look he gave her when he handed her the envelope of seeds Clare had been unable to plant, and that one frank conversation neither of them mentioned again.

She ruffled through the journal to more recent days and stopped, head bowed, as Charles answered her question. It was the entry from Christmas Eve. *I want to give her something. Will she think me a fool if it is Clare's seeds? Will it say what I'm trying to say and haven't the words yet? Can I- or may I - love her too?*

It was a question for the ages. Her eyes

closed in weariness and defeat. All she ever wanted to do was escape the Mercury Street Café. She hadn't planned to fall in love, not when she was simply trying to survive. But there he was, and she wanted more; she wanted him.

She glanced at the bed where Gwen slept. "In the morning I will tell you that whatever happens, you will not be alone," she whispered. "You are mine. We'll manage together."

She picked up a pencil and poised it over the page. She dated her entry April 16, 1904, and wrote in his journal, *Yes, you can love me. I won't forget Plato, but I want another cat.*

It looked supremely stupid. How could *anyone* compare an alley cat to a person? She nearly erased it, then decided to leave it there for a day or two. She could erase it later and no one would know.

She went back to her bed and tucked a portion of the nightshirt under her head. It did smell like Charles—a man's scent also fragrant with oil from wood and varnish.

Her shoulders relaxed and she slept. The wind roared on.

Seventeen

THE SILENCE WOKE her. Ellen sat up, startled, then relieved to see sunlight streaming through the gap in the curtains. She dressed quickly, still brushing her hair when she opened the door.

"We didn't want to wake you," Mrs. Quincy said as she handed the graniteware coffee pot to Mr. Wilson.

"I can help," Ellen said. "I need to keep busy."

And she did, all that day and the next, and the one after as the rescuers—nearly all the carpenters—hitched up teams and wagons to clear the road. The telephone lines were up by the third day as soldiers from Fort Yellowstone indicated they were doing the same. "We'll meet somewhere in the middle," Dan Reeves told her.

The sun shone bitter cold for two more days, then spring returned. Ellen woke to ice melting off the roof. Fickle, daunting Wyoming. She doubted the new state would ever have much population.

"We'll know more soon," Mr. Wilson told her as his road crew started out. He left behind the best carpenters to continue finishing the rooms. Mr. Reamer quietly directed Charles's work. He took Ellen aside to assure her that she would always have employment with Harry Child and the YP Company. "There's a place for you here."

She understood. No one commented about yesterday's telephone call before the line went down again. Searchers from Fort Yellowstone had found one horse dead in the Gardner River, not far from Golden Gate.

Gwen didn't need to know. She still cried herself to sleep at night, but so did Ellen, who'd told her that no matter what, she was never to worry about what would become of her. "We'll stick together," she said.

Ellen should have known that the whole

Ellen Found

terrifying ordeal would end with no fanfare, no bells, no one scattering rose petals, just the sound of the big door opening.

Gwen was more attuned to her father's footsteps than anyone. She looked up from sewing hems on napkins for summer guests. "Ellen," she said uncertainly, her eyes wide.

Then came the sound of other footsteps and Sergeant Reeves's cheery, "Guess who's home!"

Gwen ran into the lobby. Ellen followed, then sagged against the doorframe as father and daughter came together with shouts of joy. She watched in utter relief, then began a checklist. He was thin. He hadn't shaved in a week and his beard was straggly. Red eyes. The tips of his ears looked chewed up, maybe frostbitten. He was alive. She loved him.

"Got him back to you."

She took a good look at Dan Reeves, who also looked chewed up. This was the sergeant who had saved her life and hinted at marriage. "What do you mean? Don't tease."

"Just that," he said cheerfully. "We spent a night holed up with Charles and the driver. He assured me he would take good care of you. I told him I could too. He said no, that was his job."

She couldn't help a smile, her first in a week. "Thanks for getting him back alive, Dan."

"You're welcome." He looked at father and daughter. "Drat his hide! Besides, I have orders to Fort Clark, then a return to the Philippines. Orders." He kissed her cheek. "He has something else I don't have."

She gave him an inquiring look.

"He'll show you." He kissed her again and not on the cheek this time. "I told him if he didn't take good care of you, I'd know. God bless you both, Ellen."

She turned to see Charles set his daughter down and whisper to her. Gwen skipped into the kitchen, calling, "Mrs. Quincy, he's really hungry!"

Sergeant Reeves gave her a push in Charles's direction, then headed for the kitchen. In another moment she was held tight by a man who needed food, a bath, and a shave. She felt his breath against her neck. She kissed him at precisely the same moment he had the

Ellen Found

same notion, then tightened her hands across his back, pulling him close.

His week-old beard scratched her face; she didn't care. "All I could think of was you," he said finally. "I froze and starved and realized that I have a big heart with room for others. I know you want to be a front desk clerk here, but I'd rather you married me instead. I love you."

Gwen gestured to them from the dining room. "Coming in a minute, Daughter," Charles said. "I went to Butte for the machinery, not Bozeman," he said as the others left the lobby. "The Mercury Street Café burned down a month ago."

"Too bad it wasn't sooner," she said, then gasped, "*Really?*"

"Who jokes about that? I found a souvenir for you in the alley though. Put your hand in my overcoat pocket."

It was one thing to agree to marriage, but Ellen was proper. She shook her head.

"Knothead! Do it."

She pulled out a kitten who looked deep into her eyes, then cocked its head, as if wanting to know her better.

"I named him Socrates. When pickings got slim there at Golden Gate, I told him that he would eat when I did and starve with me, too."

"I told Plato that," she said softly.

"Socrates shared some of his canned milk, but I am never going to like sardines."

They sat down close together, hips touching, Ellen content to cuddle Socrates. She watched her man wolf down apple pie and nod when the cook brought in a bowl of stew. He shared his bowl with the kitten, which turned Ellen's vision misty.

Soon the dining room filled with workers, listening as Charles told of cold nights and days wrapped in blankets and rugs intended for the inn and burning some of the furniture for warmth. "I wouldn't wish that ordeal on anyone," he said simply.

"You must write about it, Da." Gwen ran into the room she shared with Ellen and returned with her father's journal. "I kept this close. Do you mind?"

"Not at all." He glanced at Ellen. "Did you read any of it?"

She nodded and spoke softly to him

alone. "I understand your love for Clare. I will never intrude on your memories."

"They're wonderful memories," he told her, his lips close to her ear, "but I live in the present."

Ellen remembered. She took the journal from him and turned to the last entry, hers. "I added this. I forgot to erase it. I was presumptuous."

"Let's see. This is mine: 'Can I- or may I- love her, too?'" He pointed to Ellen's penciled addition and nodded. "'April 16, 1904. Yes, you can love me. I won't forget Plato, but I want another cat.'"

He nodded, his tired eyes brighter. "Precisely. How about you get an ink pen and make this permanent? You know, like us."

Epilogue

IN THAT ODD way of Wyoming weather, spring sidled in when everyone was hammering, installing windows, and worrying if the final load of furniture would arrive on time. Builders and staff discovered a dismaying amount of final projects even the best of planners seem to leave undone until the end, because it was the Big Stuff that mattered.

May roared in with wind and more snow, and then suddenly, silence, followed by the steady drip of ice from the Inn's enormous sloping roof. One day the landscape was gray, and the next day that impossible green of tender buds and grass. Even the geysers, paint pots, and hot springs seemed to perk up, as if aware that this inn at Old Faithful was destined for greatness.

Ellen Found

Spring exited ahead of schedule in mid-May, as the string quartet practiced, the dining room acquired spotless white tablecloths, and rugs went down in the lobby. On his latest visit, Harry Child pronounced his project worthy of the nation's first national park.

The days lengthened and warmed like a benediction. Ellen worked long hours too, rationing her love for Charles Penrose to quick kisses in the morning and maybe a moment in the evening by the roaring fireplace in the lobby, holding hands. What else was needed? She knew her own mind.

Then came her final visit to Plato's grave outside the kitchen door, peaceful under the over-hang of windows. "I wish you could see the inn," she told him, after looking around to make sure she was alone. She patted the grave, grateful beyond measure for the little Butte stray with the courage of a mountain lion. "I'll be back now and then," she promised. "I will."

The U.S. Army triumphed. Major Pitcher knew of a frustrated Presbyterian minister in Gardiner about to leave that town of wicked sinners, and persuaded him to come to Old Faithful for a wedding. Ellen Found and

Charles Penrose were married May 30 in the lobby of Mr. Reamer's amazing inn by Old Faithful, which erupted when Ellen said, "I do." Everyone laughed.

Harry Child himself handed her new husband the key to Room 140, the final guest room at the end of the hall. "It's secluded," he confided, which made Charles blush. Gwen and Socrates stayed that night with Mrs. Wilson, the former Mrs. Quincy, who had married Mr. Wilson a week earlier. Fort Yellowstone had a federal judge who'd done the honors.

In the morning they were packed and ready to take a freight wagon to Lake Hotel, where Mr. Reamer was halfway through a remodel of that grand old dame. "I need an expert's finish work," he said, then promised Charles the lead carpenter position on the new Yellowstone Park Transportation Company barn in Gardiner. "I have more projects," he told him. "You'll be busy."

Eating leftover cake in the lobby, Mr. Child asked Ellen how she and Charles enjoyed the string quartet serenade last night outside Room 140. The violinists were still getting used to their summer job of playing for guests during dinner and dances. "I hope they impressed you," he said.

"You mean those rascals who played 'Brahms' Lullaby'?" Charles asked. His wife blushed.

And here was Sergeant Reeves, splendid in his dress uniform, but looking forlorn. Ellen leaned against Charles and his arms automatically went around her. "Dan, thanks for getting him back to me safely."

He glared at her new husband, then gave a philosophical shrug. "Drat the man, what could I do?"

"What you did."

Ellen looked around, admiring the work of a winter and knowing she would never tire of it. The first tourists were arriving tomorrow. Some projects remained undone, but it would all happen. She watched Adelaide Child instructing a pretty young thing behind the front desk. Hmm.

"Dan, go meet that front desk clerk," she said. "You look impressive right now."

He laughed at that and followed her gaze. "Yes, ma'am!"

"Will I like Lake Hotel?" she asked Charles, who watched Dan strut away.

"Yes, Mrs. Penrose, if you like cuddling with me on the front steps to watch the sun go down over the lake. It's a far cry from Mercury Street."

She relaxed in his arms. "True, but everything in my life, including Mercury Street and even Butte, brought me right here." She whispered in his ear. "Let's reserve Room 140 next year."

"Without the string quartet." He kissed the top of her head. "I've been thinking about your former name. Ellen Found. What did you find, dear heart?"

What indeed? They walked outside to look at the geyser field, ready for summer and tourists. "You, most certainly," she said. She knew his heart.

"What else?"

"Me."

ABOUT CARLA KELLY

What to say about Carla? The old girl's been in the writing game for mumble-mumble years. She started out with short stories that got longer and longer until— poof!— one of them turned into a novel. (It wasn't quite that simple.) She still enjoys writing short stories, one of which is before you now. Carla writes for Harlequin Historical, Camel Press, and Cedar Fort. Her books are found in at least 14 languages.

Along the way, Carla's books and stories have earned a couple of Spur Awards from Western Writers of America for Short Fiction, a couple of Rita Awards from Romance Writers of America for Best Regency, and a couple of Whitney Awards. Carla lives in Idaho Falls, Idaho, and continues to write, because her gig is historical fiction, and that never gets old.

Follow Carla on Facebook: Carla Kelly
Carla's Website: www.CarlaKellyAuthor.com

www.ingramcontent.com/pod-product-compliance
Lightning Source LLC
LaVergne TN
LVHW021821060526
838201LV00058B/3468